Event in the Marshes

in the

Marshes

And Other Stories

ASA LATEEF

authorHOUSE®

AuthorHouse™ UK
1663 Liberty Drive
Bloomington, IN 47403 USA
www.authorhouse.co.uk
Phone: 0800 047 8203 (Domestic TFN)
         +44 1908 723714 (International)

Published by AuthorHouse 10/16/2019

ISBN: 978-1-7283-9478-7 (sc)
ISBN: 978-1-7283-9477-0 (e)

Library of Congress Control Number: 2019916421

Print information available on the last page.

Any people depicted in stock imagery provided by Getty Images are
models, and such images are being used for illustrative purposes only.
Certain stock imagery © Getty Images.

Cover photo credit: "Courtesy of Meethaq Naeem"

This book is printed on acid-free paper.

Contents

For Heide, the one with a childlike heart who read the manuscript, wept, cared, and gave me an enormous amount of support.

And
For my children: Maytham, Amna and Yosr who sailed with me across perilous seas.

Event in the Marshes

1

It was sunset. The extensive marsh—encased in vibrant hues and interspersed with darkened patches of tubular plants, their tips shimmering in the scarlet light—looked grotesque. The waterscape presented a romantic air and a surreal touch. The sun had imperceptibly plunged with a dying blaze, leaving the oblique heaven with interlaced fading blue and crimson red that passed softly into a lilac sky. In that extinguished world where all earthly objects had become blurry and muddled, a solitary *mash-houf*[1] glided over the stagnant waters through a winding passage among the dense thickets of reeds and sedges. It was steered by a barefooted woman who stood on the narrow rear deck. Her body swayed to and fro in rhythm with the movement of the long *mardie*[2] that she used, laboriously but skilfully, to make her way through the dark waters along a meandering, forking path.

---

[1] A *mash-houf* is a light boat used in the marshes of southern Iraq.
[2] A *mardie* is a long pole used to navigate in shallow water.

The navigable serpentine passage widened and narrowed frequently, and it took the form of a small pool wherever it gained width. In such a setting, the boat generated faint parabolic wavelets and ripples that finally collided and dissipated against the bordering long reed stalks. For the most part, the course was tight, and the reeds encroached upon the waterway, rendering navigation an arduous labour that made the woman gasp for air. She had sun-baked skin, a worn-out countenance, and a grave, wrinkled face. Her lips were rough and cracked. A prominent dark blue tattoo marked her forehead, which branched over her eyebrows to extend slightly to her temples. A golden nose ornament, a *khizzama*, with a pale blue stone rested on her left nostril. Her hands were astonishingly strong and lumpy with palms that were covered with calluses—a sign of no other than a lifetime of hard work. She wore a large black turban with one dangling end hanging over her heaving chest. Her whole body was shrouded in black garments, well fastened at the waist, leaving nothing exposed but her grooved face, her veiny hands, and her fissured feet. It wouldn't be possible to give an accurate estimation of her age, as women in this forgotten land aged before their time as a result of early marriage, early motherhood, and a hard-toiling life.

Suddenly she let out a sigh of relief and paused poling. The thick, towering reeds had finally retreated, ·giving way to a spacious open marsh. The light boat slackened down and then came to a standstill. In that stationary position, the woman pulled the mardie out of the water, rested its end on the boat bottom, and Leant on it while gazing forward. Her heavy eyelashes winked rapidly, struggling against the stinging sweat that dripped into her dark eyes, blurring her vision. She held the loose end of the turban, dried her face, and then looked again. The view became clearer, and a second wave of relief flooded her exhausted face as she captured the sight of bright small fires and the diminutive floating dwellings of Haj Raisan village. It was an irregular cluster of scattered shabby *saraief*[3] constructed on platforms of craftily woven rushes known as *chebash*. In that blazing sunset, the village looked like a petrified mythical sea fleet. The silhouettes of the grey-ochre-toned dwellings were mirrored on the reddened water as colossal fading shadows.

The smoke, which densely curled up from the fires, impregnated the air with the peculiar smell of burnt water buffalo dung. Burning dung at sunset was an indispensable practice done by the people of the marshes to get rid of armies of biting mosquitoes that rendered the evenings on this waterscape an intolerable, hellish existence. This transitional time between day and night had the paradoxical combination of attenuated activity and amplified voices and sounds. It was the time when the mooing of the water buffalo, which were swimming home from their grazing grounds; the quacking of the domesticated ducks; and the children's voices acquired their most intense and pervasive effect. The boatwoman poled on again and slowly neared the floating abodes. With an air of familiarity, she steered her way towards two isolated huts on the western side of the village. Her arrival made a stir in the population, particularly

---

[3] *Saraief* are huts with low arches and inclined roofs constructed from reeds, mats, and mud.

the children, who came running joyfully towards the edge of water, accompanied by fierce barking dogs. The ill-dressed, barefooted, and shaggy boys and girls lined up along the land's edge like a badly organised reception chorus and curiously watched the newcomer gliding farther westward.

The turbaned woman carefully directed the mash-houf, which obliquely nosed in towards the muddy bank. She manoeuvred a little to align the light vessel with the grassy shore, and the boat soon came to a standstill. The woman didn't leave immediately. Her eyes were fixed upon the agitated, barking big dog that faced her. She didn't dare set foot on land, choosing to remain on the deck. At that moment, a man appeared at the dark entrance of the nearby hut. He glanced briefly then headed towards the waiting woman. He was a thin elderly man of medium stature with stooped shoulders and a yellow complexion, undoubtedly the effect of jaundice. He wore long, loose, dark grey garments, dishdasha, and covered his head with a dotted black and white headcloth, yashmak, which was crested by an *ukal*.[4] The man came limping while waving a cane in his hand. He hushed the dog in a hoarse voice: "Shut up, fool! Don't you recognise our guest?"

The furious dog instantly obeyed his master. The barking dwindled to a low growl, then it passed to deep panting. The dog squatted on his hindlimbs and watched the woman now with tamed curiosity. The man drew nearer, and his good-natured face showed a

---

[4] A *ukal* is a planispiral cord made of plaited wool or hair and comes mostly in the colour black. It is an item of men's headwear.

wide and welcoming smile that exposed his discoloured teeth. "Welcome, Zaira Tiswahen![5] Welcome!" he received the woman with his gravelly voice.

"Peace upon you, Zair abū Hasna,"[6] she replied with a low voice, avoiding eye contact with the man.[7] For years Zaira Tiswahen had led an itinerant existence. She was a boat peddler travelling through the vast region of Hor al-Hammar—the extensive marshes of southern Iraq. Her peculiar goods of mirrors, perfumes, camphor, rosaries, wooden combs, candies, buttons, needles, thread bobbins, hairpins, bracelets, and the like carried the flavour and wonders of distant towns. She got her merchandise from peripheric small towns. From there she criss-crossed Hor al-Hammar, travelling from al-Howair and al-Mdaina in the east to al-Fohoud in the west, and from Suq al-Shioukh in the south to al-Dawaya in the north. Each voyage would take her days, even weeks, and when daylight dwindled, she spent her nights at the nearest village.

---

[5] *Zaira* and *zair* are titles of respect for a woman and a man, respectively. Basically the title is acquired when the person undergoes pilgrimage to the shrine of Imam Ridha in Mashhad, Iran.

[6] According to tradition, and as a show of respect, people usually don't call each other by their first names. Rather, they address each other as "mother of ..." or "father of ...", followed by the name of the eldest child. Therefore, "abū" stands for "father of", and "umm" stands for "mother of". "Hasna" stands for the name of the daughter. However, one can call someone by his or her name when such a person has no children, like Zaira Tiswahen.

[7] It is not socially acceptable for a woman to set her eyes directly on a man who is not a close relative.

This peripatetic life was peculiar and unique, having been triggered by a happening that occurred early in her life. When did that happening occur? She herself was unable to tell as she had lost track of the sequence of days, months, and years. Her feeling for the arrow of time was limited by what she recognised of physical and tangible changes that occurred in people and things. Even with the absence of a chronological yardstick, what befell her was deeply engraved in her mind. It was the epoch of the outbreak of the devastating cholera epidemic, which claimed thousands of lives, including those of her husband and their three children. She couldn't demystify the fact of her avoidance of that destiny, but she pitied this exemption. She had always felt pathetic for being spared to outlast her loved ones. She was young back then, in her early twenties, but her social trauma incited her to escape—to wander and subconsciously try to diffuse the inner tension that led her to adopt this transient lifestyle.

2

After being assured that the hostile dog had been calmed, Zaira Tiswahen dared to set her feet on the ground. She started unloading her merchandise, which was packed in small- and medium-sized hand-sewn cloth bags. Soon she heard an affable womanly voice that she recognised well. She straightened and turned around with a genial expression on her face. The man, who was still standing aside, watched the gaunt figure of his wife approaching. She came forward and welcomed Zaira Tiswahen with open arms. Abū Hasna nodded with appreciation, then turned around and moved back towards the dark entrance of the hut.

"Welcome, Zaira Tiswahen," said umm Hasna, but with unmistakable sad tone. Her face was fraught with sadness as if she has been struck by affliction, and her eyes averted the visitor's gaze. Zaira Tiswahen hurried to lay down the bag she held in her hands and advanced to embrace the welcoming woman. "Dear umm Hasna, how are you?" she asked in a concerned tone. "Welcome, welcome Zaira Tiswahen," repeated the other woman in a soft and quavering voice. She kissed her guest's sun-baked cheek.

The boatwoman returned the kiss with one of her own and kept holding umm Hasna's lanky body to her chest. There was a brief silence, during which there was indistinct sobbing.

"There is a sort of sorrow—" umm Hasna admitted, but immediately diverted course. "Come on in and have a rest. There is enough time to talk later." She hurried to help with the merchandise bags, after which both women walked into the low reed house.

By now, the moribund glow of the vanishing sun made its final manifestation on the darkened waters, then abruptly duskiness cloaked the world. Stillness reigned. Except for the distant sound of a melodious double-reed pipe, the silence was total and comprehensive. Inside the hut, the accumulating darkness was partially driven out by one pressurised kerosene mantle lantern hanging from a reed-woven pole in the middle of the guest room or *raba'a*. In the back room, there was a kerosene lantern and an oil lamp hanging at two opposite sides of the reed-mat walls. The two compartments of the hut were separated by a low-lying partition clay wall with an overhanging faded colour curtain. The interaction of darkness and the flickering light drew on the walls and ceiling gigantic quivering shadows of people and things. Zaira Tiswahen passed through the arched entrance and caught sight of four men sitting in the spacious raba'a. She offered a courteous greeting and continued her way together with umm Hasna to the inner living room.

The shabby light of the family dwelling exposed the scene of a young girl stretched on a bed set on the floor. She was Hasna, the daughter of Zaira Tiswahen's hosts. Her emaciated body was imperceptibly shivering, and the tenuous light made her pallid complexion even paler. Her body was bathed in sweat, and her sunken eyes were surrounded by dark haloes. She was mumbling inscrutable words—like someone with delirium. Zaira Tiswahen was shocked by what she saw. The decline of the physique of Hasna, a once lovely, vibrant girl, was so precipitous that it brought her the shadow of a distant painful picture, which startled her. She crouched beside the head of the semicomatose girl, held her hand that bore a green ribbon, an *alag*,[8] and kissed her wet forehead. "What is the matter with Hasna? Why is she so pallid and weak?" Zaira Tiswahen enquired while sitting herself on a small square cushion that her host has just provided. The mother didn't answer immediately as she was keen first to serve her visitor. She moved to the nearby

---

[8] An alag is a sort of fetish. It is a green cloth band that has been rubbed against a holy tomb with the belief that it has the power to heal.

mahmal,[9] took from it a new cylindrical iridescent cushion, and put it beside her guest to rest her elbow. Then she opened a small wooden chest with copper ornaments, took out a cylindrically wrapped bundle of Mzabban[10] cigarettes and a match, and sat beside her guest.

"She suddenly got sick out of nowhere. It commenced with fatigue and loss of appetite," The mother sighed and lit a cigarette for her companion. "It all started a short time after your last visit, and since then her health has declined rapidly," she said. She fought back her tears and added, "Her sickness has baffled us."

Zaira Tiswahen blinked a little as the smoke of her cigarette spiralled up to the tubular ceiling. She listened attentively, remaining silent for few moments. "Haven't you taken her to Sayyid Dekheel?"[11] she thoughtfully asked.

"Oh, Zaira! There is nothing that can be done which we have not done. We even brought al-Arfa[12] from Fawada, who supplied her with *tamima*,[13] but it was in vain. No medicine that we know helped her. We are helpless ..." the lamenting mother said in a despairing voice that

---

[9] A mahmal is a piece of wooden multipurpose furniture that normally serves as a container and holder of the family's fine articles, mattresses, pillows, bed sheets, etc. It is ornamented and usually is set with a mirror in the middle.
[10] Mzabban is a brand of local cigarette with a tubular mouthpiece that lacks a filter.
[11] A local holy shrine.
[12] An *arfa* is a woman of traditional knowledge who helps local people with medical and related metaphysical cures. Fawada is a village to the south-south-west of the marshes.
[13] A tamima is a wonder-working icon.

9

immediately metamorphosed into silent weeping. Zaira Tiswahen, sorely perplexed, released a sound that was a mixture of a sigh and a moan. She flicked the ashes of her cigarette on the floor while exhaling the smoke through her nostrils. Lost for words, Zaira Tiswahen rested her elbow on her raised right knee and stared with a troubled look at the sick girl through the whirling rarefied smoke that kept seeping from her nose.

The scene before her eyes conjured up the image of her dying children a long time ago. The tragic memories of the bereaved woman rushed out of her subconscious mind, vivid and tormenting. A long time ago she had developed a saddening trait, a sort of psychological symptom, that whenever she encountered a severely sick juvenile, she would feel the dark shadows of an evil portent. For a while, she sagely repressed her dispirited mood and uttered a few soothing words, but soon after she assumed a brooding appearance; she was really despondent of what she thought would be the inevitable woeful outcome.

Presently she had finished her cigarette, and her eyes met those of umm Hasna. *What can be done to alleviate the grief of my friend?* her fluttering mind wondered. And then, out of her bafflement, she said, "Look here, dear umm Hasna." She pulled from her waist a tiny thing wrapped in a piece of dark cloth. "I'd put this tested talisman under the pillow of Hasna. It would do her good." Her voice came with an encouraging tone. She extended her hand and inserted the talisman beneath the head of the unconscious girl. The mother, desperate and fatigued, thanked her guest for this initiative, and after a certain exchange of words and receiving news from her guest about other villages, umm Hasna excused herself to start preparing the supper at the other end of the room. Left alone, the emotions of Zaira Tiswahen came unharnessed. She silently sobbed with a heaving breast. Rills of teardrops, mixed with kohl[14] from her eyelashes, rolled down her weather-beaten face. She looked at the girl, pulled out a large, pale blue handkerchief from her side pocket, and bent over the sick girl to wipe her profusely sweating face.

The bed on which the sick girl was lying was next to a low circular window. During the evenings, this porthole-like opening looked like a patch of black communicating with the nocturnal world. During the daytime it revealed an expanse of stagnant waters interspersed by scattered tall reeds. The small window was constructed to allow the passage of a breeze to refresh the poorly aerated dwelling. One such rare movement of air suddenly occurred and stirred the stagnant air of the back room. It was a slight air current, but it was enough, when it feathered the face of the girl, to cause a movement of her eyelids. There was even some slight movement of her wasted body on the thin, feather-stuffed mattress.

It was a moonless, starry night, and the sky was embellished with a myriad of twinkling stars, causing a whitish stellar glow to run across the firmament. Undoubtedly, this same enrapturing scene had fascinated Shaba'ad[15] and countless dreamy girls of Mesopotamia over the millennia. But for the turbulent mind of Hasna, the view looked fuzzy and

---

[14] Kohl is a traditional eye cosmetic.
[15] Shaba'ad or Shubad is a Sumerian Akkadian priestess, a queen from the first dynasty of Ur (*c.*2550 BC).

11

incomprehensible. The bright dots of the sky seemed to her troubled eyes as luminous dancing spheres of ever changeable diameters, spheres that expanded and contracted then merged to separate again, the process repeating itself incessantly. She felt herself afloat and dizzy, and her ears captured obscured, muffled voices. Her body wrestled to turn around to face the direction from which the indiscriminate voices came. Through misty, half-open eyes, she saw darkness smeared with patches of faint light. She strained her eyes to focus on the bleary sight that was unfolding before her. Firstly, she saw the outlines of the person sitting nearby her, the turbaned woman, and next she recognised the bending figure of her mother at the far end of the room.

Zaira Tiswahen, who up to that moment had been watching her host cooking in the corner, turned around to check on the girl. With a surprised look she observed the partial return of awareness to the girl and let out a sound of relief that didn't escape the hearing of the busy mother, who instantly came, at a rapid pace, and sat at the head of her daughter. With an encouraging smile and brightened eyes, the mother extended a rough hand and gently massaged the head of her withered daughter. "Oh, my dear! Oh, my lovely daughter!" she uttered as she bent over, caressing and kissing her child while simultaneously weeping.

Zaira Tiswahen, on her part, observed the dull and contracted eyes of the girl, but she overcame her growing worries and bent to kiss her warm forehead. "How are you, my dear? Do you feel better?" the solemn guest asked in a caring tone, but the incapacitated girl remained silent. Her dry, cracked lips were partially arched, exposing two rows of small white teeth that were intermittently chattering. Zaira Tiswahen reached behind her neck and loosened a cord bearing a single sky-blue stone[16] with seven perforations. "Here is an additional thing that could support the other talisman and protect Hasna from all evil," she said with an internal feeling lacking in resonant confidence. The mother nodded approvingly and gently raised the head of her daughter while the other woman wrapped the fetish cord around the neck of the girl. By virtue of these movements, Hasna regained more of her senses. Her ears captured a fluctuating, droning sound, which sounded in her turbid mind like the distant thudding of the Haj Badran mill in al-Fohoud.[17] Then the thudding passed gradually into indistinct humming that finally became intermingled human voices coming from the raba'a. The girl's failing body and depleted mind couldn't allow her further recognition, and once more she closed her eyes to slip into a dazed half slumber. With this, the mother's face became overcast again. Both despondence and hope slithered elusively in her mind, but her motherhood pressed for hope. She turned her face upwards, raised her hands, and with a suppliant tone and transcendental impetus she beseeched, "Oh God, save my daughter!" Then she collapsed into silent weeping.

Zaira Tiswahen, with a thwarted heart, wrapped umm Hasna in her arms and pressed her tightly, trying to calm her down. "Be hopeful. Be hopeful, please."

---

[16] The blue stone with seven "eyes" is thought to have the power to shatter evil into seven parts, and hence the evil loses its power. Some researchers think that this superstitious belief has its roots in ancient Babylonian spiritual beliefs.

[17] Al-Fohoud is a district on the south-west margin of the marshes.

3

The four men in the raba'a sat on a plaited yellow reed mat, a *baria*, covered by light colour-banded rugs. Small, cylindrical, feather-stuffed pillows that were slipped into pale blue satin cloth cases and adorned with braided rope trims at both ends were laid transversally to serve as armrests. Three of the four men conversed sombrely with each other, while the fourth, the youngest member of the group, listened attentively. The host, abū Hasna, with pitying looks and a slight tremble to his hands, was on his feet holding a number of small nested finely ornamented porcelain cups in one hand and a soot-tainted brass pot in the other, ready to serve his guests the sour coffee. Next to the host's empty place sat abū Jawda, an immediate neighbour with peculiar mottled skin and a hairless face, giving him an illusory youthful complexion. He had slanted eyes and partially parted lips exposing gapped teeth, which gave him a somewhat imbecilic aspect. His fingers were busy, moving in a fast and nervous manner, with the beads of his *misbaha*[18] as he listened to the other companion, the one who looked to be the most prominent member of the group. He was Sayyid Majeed, the clergyman, and the most influential and respected person in the region. He always dressed in nifty perfumed garments that contrasted with the shabby clothing of the villagers. But, as would become clear later, that sartorial distinction was just one of the facets that distinguished the man. His hefty body, which was quite a rare physical feature among the people of

---

[18] Islamic prayer beads.

14

the area, was shrouded by a light black abaya.[19] He covered his head with a unique black *yashmagh*, and a green scarf hung around his neck. These two garments of black and green colours manifested his special religious status as sayyid.[20] With a flabby body, a rosy glow on his face, and soft skin, he assumed another peculiar aspect that spoke of good health and an easy-going lifestyle, uncommon in that harsh environment. Indeed, he relished good food! And seldom did he miss any of the festivities or savoury meals that were relatively abundant all year round. His round face had dark oval eyes crowned by a bushy monobrow, while his puffy cheeks were partially covered by a thick black beard, which in turn sandwiched a pug nose. He sat on a white fleece, and from that distinct and privileged seat, his gaze glistened with authority.

The overdone sober air that he surrounded himself with and his condescending character did have some basis in the fact of things, though. He was the only person in the whole region who was able to read and write; he was an orator endowed with a fervid eloquence who performed the annual religious rituals of Ashura.[21] These abilities and characteristics of the clergyman had established his reverence and

---

[19] An abaya is a loose cloak-like garment.

[20] Sayyid is a title given to a person who is thought to be a descendant of Prophet Muhammad.

[21] Ashura literally means the tenth of Muharram (the first month of the Hijri calendar). On Ashura, Shia Muslims annually mourn the martyrdom of Imam Husain on this date in the sixty-first year Hijri. Mourning takes place during the first ten days of Muharram and extends to the twentieth of the next month, Safar.

authoritative influence in this remote isolated society that was virtually illiterate.

The fourth, and youngest, man was Hameed. He looked detached from the others and lost in his pondering. He was the cousin and fiancé[22] of the sick girl. An orphan nephew of abū Hasna, he lived with his aging grandmother on the other edge of the village. The humbly clad youth wore a dishdasha of faded grey corduroy and enfolded his head with a dull white kofia. His tanned hairless face, except for a thin moustache and a few scattered hairs on his chin, showed a perplexed expression. He did not take part in the sombre discussion that was going on among the three elderly men, though he kept listening intently to their lengthy study of Hasna's illness, which discussion eventually came to a standstill as a restless silence fell over the men. That was the time when abū Hasna started to serve coffee for his guests. The basic question, which concerned the cure of Hasna, remained unsettled. Hameed, who had hoped for a breakthrough in the crisis, became edgy and impatient with the incompleteness of the talk and immediately found himself submerged in ramified thoughts that chaotically roved across a vast field of imminent challenges and past memories. He tried to find meaning in the swirling and nonorchestrated thoughts, but his attempts were in vain.

When he heard his uncle, during the foregoing round of talks, repeatedly saying that they had exhausted all means to heal Hasna, Hameed defiantly

---

[22] According to social traditions, the masculine cousin (on the father's side) has priority to marry his female cousin.

shook his head because he did not consider that to be the final word. "There should be a solution, a cure," he said insistently to convince himself. It was torment for the young man to admit despair or incapacity. The tug of war between his defiance and the absence of a solution steered him to withdraw into himself, where he found solace in his memories. He retrospectively conjured up past events and poignantly recollected joyous social moments, particularly the feast days, the ornamented boat trains that criss-crossed the marshes, the barrage of celebratory salvos of rifles, and above all Hasna—Hasna in her charming corduroy yellow dress embellished with fine red roses and sky-blue ciliated ribbons, trimmed with shining silvery lace. For him, the jubilant feasts and Hasna were inseparable things, two faces of the same coin of happiness and glamour. In his heart and mind there were plenty of pleasant memories, great aspirations, and big dreams, and life, under the effect of the magical chemistry of love, seemed to flow agreeably and timelessly beyond and above the limits and restrictions of real life.

But now, reality struck him mercilessly. Hasna was lying down nearby, a mere skeleton, a yellow phantom pleading for life, while he was sitting helpless and powerless. He Leant his back against the reedy wall, away from the direct light of the lantern, as if attempting to hide his stigmatising aspect from the eyes of the elderly company. During that time of frustrating muteness, the distressed father, abū Hasna, thought it was good to serve another round of coffee for his guests, so he set off again, with cracked hands, to pour the black liquid into the tiny cups.

Meanwhile, abū Jawda kept looking, open-mouthed,

at the face of Sayyid Majeed, who assumed a stately appearance and a meditative expression, waiting for him to break that inconclusive silence. The clergyman, who intensified his occult gestures, which had been crafted during his long career as an orator, was capable of maintaining his mystic influence even in the absence of verbal communication. His obscure signs and inscrutable ways, though bogus and theatrical by their very nature—an actuality that wouldn't, of course, be uncovered by these people—had nevertheless immense reassuring effects on his audience during times of stress, a reality proving that utility outweighs truth. However, at this particular moment, the contemplative silence of Sayyid Majeed had a purpose; it was a precursor for something specific and important that he was mulling over. He bent his head slightly downward while his fingers played with the beads of the black misbaha. Then he raised his head again and looked at the men, who were waiting with expectancy. The white of his eyes floated and shone in such a way as if he were experiencing some sort of divine revelation. Finally, and to the great relief of the men, the obese clergyman turned his head towards the poor father, abū Hasna, and slowly opened his lips to speak with an air of abstruseness, in the manner of someone divulging a great and precious secret. "Abū Hasna! There is one way to save your daughter," he said, pausing to gulp his coffee in one go while his eyes surveyed the faces of the men, who instantly became galvanised by the spoken words. Hameed emerged from his seclusion as his ears caught the scanty words. He curiously stared at the sayyid's puffy face.

The other two men looked extremely excited.

The more prompted of the two was the father, abū Hasna, who uttered something like "Wa ..." in a disharmonious high pitch. Apparently, he'd started to ask "What?" but then stopped short of completing his enquiry as he remained, together with abū Jawda, impatiently waiting for the clergyman to elaborate.

Sayyid Majeed, satisfied by the impact of his introductory statement, continued in his characteristic clipped tone: "Yes, there is but one unique possibility to cure untreatable illness like the one that afflicts your girl!" He kept a straight face while his thumb and forefinger slipped in a slow and rhythmic manner over the large beads of his misbaha.

"And what is it? God bless you, Sayyid," came the begging voice of the wistful father.

"It is an esoteric prescription that was handed down to me by my father, mercy upon him, and which he had inherited from his sada[23] ancestors long ago," the clergyman said. With this enigmatic statement, an awesome feeling surrounded the men.

The grieved father, still captured by the awe-inspiring words of Sayyid Majeed, enquired in a pleading tone, "And what is this medicine, Sayyid?"

"It is not a medicine but a cure," corrected the confident voice. For abū Hasna, as well as for the other two men, the reply was an obscure clarification, a conundrum that drew a mixture of perplexity and eagerness to their faces.

Abū Jawda carelessly jabbed his cigarette, and the ashes fell on the carpet. Then with a hoarse voice, he echoed the single question that resonated in the heads

---

[23] *Sada* is the plural of *sayyid*.

of the others. "What is it, Sayyid? What is this cure?" he asked impatiently and gaped in bewilderment, which caused his inveterate imbecilic looks to appear at their utmost.

"It is an apparition having divine curing effects," the clergyman started, still embodying too much ambiguity to be easily followed by his listeners. His tone and facial expression indicated that what he was about to convey to his listeners was unique knowledge reserved for the most elite and the most erudite. Abū Jawda, with a dropped jaw and arched eyebrows, had not yet received an answer to his question, so he kept his inquisitive expression.

Abū Hasna was no less confused than his neighbour. By crawling on all fours, he came closer to Sayyid Majeed. He squatted beside him and looked at the rounded stern face. "Sayyid, what do you mean by … Oh, what was that?" He seemed at a loss for a moment, and he'd spoken his last statement as if talking to himself. Then he stuttered, "Ah, the *appartition*?" He said this and immediately realised his improper pronunciation, so he scratched his head and continued in an embarrassed tone, "Excuse my ignorance, but I do not understand!" He Leant forward, craving for an answer. Until that moment, Hameed had not moved a limb, but when the talk reached that point, he too dragged himself nearer to the clergyman. He sat there cross-legged, rested his elbows on his knees, supported his chin with both palms, and waited with curiosity for further elucidation.

"Apparition, abū Hasna! Apparition!" Sayyid Majeed corrected with condescending gestures. Then he went on explaining in a potent voice: "It is an ancestral knowledge, a sacred legacy that tells of how a unique divine miracle could happen that would provide a cure for the incurable." He paused for a moment, during which time abū Hasna, with increasing impatience, hurried to fill the empty cup of Sayyid Majeed with the heavy warm liquid.

The stout man slowly sipped his coffee and glanced at abū Hasna. "I am revealing this for the first time," he said with an air of charity and bestowal of favour. Then he moved his eyes towards the others and added, "Now, listen carefully." The three men, being on very high alert, held their breath in anticipation of what would be revealed next. "In the case of an incurable disease, the Divinity might intervene with a specific miracle to heal the terminally ill person," he said, his eyes shining with a hypnotising metallic lustre.

"And how is that? How that could be?" abū Hasna pleaded. The clergyman did not immediately answer; instead, his eyes shifted obliquely past his companions and upward, towards the low dark ceiling, in a gesture suggesting he was in communication with the heavens above.

"The miracle will happen, by His permission and His clemency, at dawn. In the dim twilight of dawn, a real corporeal vision of a holy wali[24] will appear within sight of the sick person," he said, his face assuming an arcane expression. "The wali will appear poling a boat, dressed in white, with a slain wild boar lying at his feet." He paused for a moment, after which he delivered the remarkable conclusion: "The phenomenal sight of the

---

[24] A wali is a holy person privileged with the ability to perform miraculous deeds.

wali will ensure the healing of the hopeless disease. In this case I refer to Hasna." The clergyman, fully aware of the deep impact of his outlandish speech on his listeners, rolled his eyes and then partially closed them as if he were in spiritual ecstasy. The men, upon hearing the succinct, eccentric revelation, fell into bewilderment and entrancement. There were a few moments of deep silence.

Then, abū Hasna, charged by a surging wave of hope and relief, exclaimed, "Blessed be the womb that bore you, Sayyid."

On his part, abū Jawda was deeply affected by what he had heard, and superstitious awe invaded his heart. His unsettled facial expression gave the clear sign of someone who could not fully accommodate what had been said. His eyes roamed over his companions as if searching for support to give meaning to the exotic talk of Sayyid Majeed. *He is the most knowledgeable who ever walked on two legs,* abū Jawda thought to himself as he stole a glance at the self-exalted clergyman.

Hameed, with a soul flitting between hope and despair, was taken by astonishment that soon transformed into meditation on what he had heard. His eyes mapped out the bulky figure in a curious manner, and then he scratched his head and perplexedly mumbled to himself, "How could such a weird thing happen?" He opened his mouth to vocalise his thoughts, but he restrained himself and remained silent. He felt a tingling limb, so he changed his posture by folding his left leg under his haunches and keeping the other knee upright, encircled by both hands. He propped his chin on the raised knee and looked to the clergyman, who was still submerged in what seemed to be a state of sublimation, in anticipation of further details.

The host, abū Hasna, feeling the burden of the prevailing silence, knelt on both knees, bent his upper body forward, and sharply inhaled some smoke from his cigarette, which he had just lit. He stared thoughtfully at Sayyid Majeed. "A slain wild boar?! Why? What significance does this have?" he enquired as if unable to concentrate but on one fragment of the bizarre tale. At that moment, the clergyman was murmuring to himself while his fingers played slowly with the beads of the misbaha. To all appearances, he seemed aloof and in another, nonearthly world, but in actuality he was watching, from his partially closed eyes, with rapture, the stunned men.

Upon hearing the question of abū Hasna, he looked at the waiting, eager face for a few moments then provided a tardy response: "A slain wild boar. It represents the eradication of evil and sickness." His voice had that usual confident tone which had always compelled his listeners to trust his words. Yet the oddity of what the three men heard was so immense that it entangled them in a cobweb of spellbound stupor as they stared, mutely, at Sayyid Majeed. But even so, the clergyman hit home. People of these isolated hinterlands were deeply superstitious with strong beliefs in myths and the supernatural. Their mindset and their psychological structure allowed them to submit uncritically to metaphysical claims. But even so, the mere possibility that a holy and untouchable entity such as the wali might dwell nearby and be among them brought cryptic awe and mystic fear. This is why the face of abū Jawda had grown pale and his startled eyes roved spasmodically over the low, dim ceiling as if in anticipation of the appearance of a ghostly creature in the dark stagnant air.

The host, abū Hasna, with an undetermined state of mind, wrinkled his forehead and intensely focused his invoking eyes on the clergyman while his body was slowly oscillating to and fro. Hameed could no longer control his amazement, and his voice came in an abrupt start as though the words had been uprooted out of him. "This is unbelievable! It is an unimaginable thing!" he exclaimed in a somewhat high-pitched voice that was certainly amplified by the prevailing silence.

Instantly a shade of resentment appeared on the face of Sayyid Majeed as he took the remark of the young man as reprehensible interjection. He looked at him askance and held up a warning finger. "Do not blaspheme! God is able to do anything at any time!" the clergyman said in absolute certitude and with an authoritative delivery that embodied his acrimonious criticism of the young man. The other two men, shocked by the notion of blasphemy, shook their heads in protest and nodded in support of Sayyid Majeed. Both cast a reproaching look at Hameed.

After the rebuke from the clergyman, a tense silence charged with dissonant feelings enwrapped the two confronting men. But the young man struggled to stifle his dudgeon and thought it was better to hold his tongue; he wasn't an ornery, pugnacious person. Yet he couldn't help but grumble to himself, "It is a pretty eccentric tale. That it is."

This instant of dispute accentuated the growing fact that Hameed didn't get on well with the clergyman; there was no love lost between the two. The frayed relationship had developed over time. After several occasions of disagreement and discordance, Sayyid Majeed had finally categorised the young man as mutinous, a maverick with perverse and unsettling thoughts that harmed the community spirit. On his part, the young man was estranged from Sayyid Majeed not only because of the arrogant air of superiority of the clergyman, his provoking facade of inerrancy, and his gorgeous rhetoric, but also because of his parasitic lifestyle, or better yet his life of stasis. He didn't work the land to grow the crops or vegetables; he didn't fish or practise a trade. His principal "activity" throughout the year was limited to the ten days of Ashura religious ceremonies, during which he delivered impassioned, lamenting speeches. But even that activity of short duration, Hameed reasoned, could hardly be called work. Furthermore, the clergyman was eligible to receive al-Khums,[25] which came from the wealthy chieftains. This provided Sayyid Majeed with a good income both in cash and in kind, which contributed to his affluence and social privileges. It also brought the notion, in Hameed's mind, that the clergyman was sponging off others, which created in the young man a lurking resentment.

The uncomfortable silence didn't last long, because after a while, abū Jawda fidgeted a little and scratched his head as though slipping into a state of thought. Then with a hesitant voice he spoke his thoughts: "Sayyid, how long should Hasna wait before she sees …"—he

---

[25] Al-Khums is for Shia Muslims an obligatory tax imposed by sharia. They must pay one-fifth of the surplus of their annual income to the sada.

paused for a moment, feeling a tremor in his body, then he breathed out his remaining words—"the wali?"

"Nobody knows!" the answer came with an unwavering tone. "It might be the first dawn or any later dawn!" Abū Jawda twisted his lips as though to put forth another enquiry, but he swallowed his saliva and remained silent. Then Sayyid Majeed added something else: "Much is dependent on divine willingness, on whether the person deserves such divine intervention." He said this soberly and scanned his companions with a penetrating gaze. Then to increase the reassuring effect, he continued, "I will pray for your daughter." He threw his arms up towards the soot-covered ceiling and uttered a few holy verses.

But Hameed had some trouble with this "cure". Like his elder companions, he was dazzled and astonished by the singularity of what he had heard. However, unlike his uncle and abū Jawda, his anxiety was not dispelled by the assertive and reassuring words of Sayyid Majeed. When the clergyman had started by indicating that there was a cure, Hameed saw a beacon of hope, but on second thought, after the disclosure of other details, he sensed that the plan wasn't airtight. As vague rational considerations surfaced in his mind, the miraculous character of the unveiled scheme ebbed and waned his initial hope. The formidable supernatural nature of what he had heard boggled his mind and caused him uneasiness. Naturally, metaphysical beliefs had been instilled in his mind. He had inherited the local culture, and this inevitably became part of his psychology, a culture suffused with superstition and, further, thoroughly mixed with religious contortions that were constantly entrenched by unscrupulous, semiliterate, expedient clergy, all of which engineered and programmed the society's collective mindset in this desolated watery world in such a way that predisposition to myths and predilection for irrational beliefs became utterly dominant. Therefore, Hameed was part of this magico-mythic tapestry. But some degree of mental change had occurred within the young man during the last two or three years. This change was so impalpable that he himself was not aware of it except for the few effects that appeared occasionally, consequently causing him social embarrassment. This metamorphosis, slow and limited as it was, was related to his new experiences that gradually made him leery of the common convictions and popular persuasions. His travels and repeated mingling with the urban society, which in and of itself was not a common occurrence for the people of the marshes in those days, brought him new world views.

Hameed worked as a guide for a foreign oil company which conducted geophysical exploration surveys in the vast swamps of the south. Accompanying scientists in their inflatable boats, Hameed found himself observing marvellous technological tools, patient observations of nature, and the neat tabulation and registration of the gained data. The sophistication of the instruments and their "magical" output of cryptic information dazed the young man and thrilled him to a great extent. He had no ability to read, and he didn't know what all these things meant; nevertheless, he was impressed by what he observed just the same. Indeed, the experience engendered curiosity in the young man. Equally important were his repeated stays in the towns of al-Qurnah, Basra, and particularly

Nasiriyah. This introduced him to different sorts of people and brought him in contact with trends of thought that were uncommon in the society of Mi'dan.[26] In Nasiriyah town particularly he encountered an effendi,[27] whom he later met several other times. This man attracted his attention, and Hameed found himself examining him and comparing him with the personality of Sayyid Majeed. The effendi was a smart, talkative person, though he lacked the soaring oratory with which Sayyid Majeed was so gifted. However, what was so different about him were the topics he talked about, which had quite different themes from those of the clergyman. The effendi, during their encounters, kept expressing to Hameed unfamiliar views on usual daily life matters, and though at times he used strange expressions, the topics were generally clear and comprehensible. He talked about the rights of peasants and the tyranny of the chieftains. He frequently mentioned the widespread illiteracy and blamed it for the spread of superstition throughout society. Indeed, the effendi called Hameed to rethink the dominant doctrines and habits which were heavily loaded with enslaving social codes, myths, and magical beliefs that became enshrouded with an unshakeable religious sacredness. Such thoughts opened the eyes of the young man to examine and question things that were considered unquestionable. They sowed in him the seeds of vigilance towards prevailing traditions.

These experiences and cultural acquisitions

---

[26] Mi'dan are the people of the marshes.

[27] Effendi is a title given to a literate man with modern attire. The word has Ottoman roots.

explained why Hameed was cautious about what Sayyid Majeed had revealed. In the deep recesses of his mind there was the troubling doubt that what Sayyid Majeed talked about was no more than a figment of the imagination. Uncertain, Hameed bowed his head, narrowed his eyes, and used his right index finger to poke the dark, soft soil.

At that time, the father had practical concerns. He cracked his knuckles and asked, "Sayyid, are there conditions for this apparition to appear?" He paused for a moment then added, "I mean conditions on the part of Hasna?"

The clergyman took his time. He rubbed his misbaha, lifted his hands, and inhaled the emanating amber smell. He lifted an index finger in warning, then answered, "The girl should be bodily in a pure state. Full ablution is required. And starting from the day of intention, she must stay awake at dawn and keep her eyes open. The rest will depend on God's will." He wriggled to keep his abaya from slipping off his shoulders.

Hameed cast a curious look at Sayyid Majeed. He wondered about this power of volubility of utterance, coupled with charismatic gestures, to sell hardly plausible claims. He was certain that all the people in the village, including Hasna, would believe in this weird prescription of Sayyid Majeed. This obsessed him. His face passed from wonderment to contemplation, and soon he acquired a brooding aspect. Absently, his hand took hold of the *megwar*[28] that was beside him

---

[28] A *megwar* is a club of wood with a rounded head of bitumen. It is used to fend off dogs and as a weapon.

and moved its wooden tip randomly over the dark face of the ground as if reflecting the haphazard path of his wandering thoughts that he couldn't assemble in a specific direction. His spirits fluctuated up and down; at one moment he felt frustration as the field of his thoughts seemed disorderly and lacking in a clear course, but at the next moment there emerged a faint glitter here and a dim glimmer there, though these scintillations faded out before acquiring a meaningful signal. However, these miniscule, ambiguous mind indications proved to be precursors of a rewarding delivery, for all of a sudden, a shrewd, bold idea emanated and brightened him up. Yes, out of the blue, Hameed got a flux of inspiration that brought him brilliant, brave, and feasible resolve that made him hopeful, vibrant, and harrowed by fervent enthusiasm. "What a scheme! I hope it works," he feverishly whispered to himself. The idea that had just popped up was astute, exciting, and brave. He grasped it without even spending a single moment of study or examination. However, because of the very nature of this inspired plan, he had to keep it to himself and clandestinely carry it out without revealing any of its element to any of the others. *I should act immediately,* he thought, and he determined to leave straightaway to prepare himself for the awaiting urgent task.

With a fluttering heart, Hameed looked in the direction of the veiled quarter where his sick fiancée lay, and then he turned his head towards his uncle. The young man appeared hesitant for a moment, then he gathered himself and talked in an undertone. "Uncle ... I ask your permission," he said, pausing for a fraction of a second as if to summon his courage. He resumed in a wavering voice, "I need to go as I have to leave early in the morning tomorrow."

When the young man delivered his words, the uncle was busy using a rusty steel rod to poke the few dying embers beneath the darkened brass coffee pot. On hearing his nephew, abū Hasna lifted his head, wiggled his shoulders with astonishment, and then, with raised eyebrows, enquired, "What did you say? Leaving early tomorrow morning? Where?"

"Well, Uncle, I know … I am terribly sorry that I didn't tell you this before." Hameed struggled to contain his embarrassment. "I would love to stay, but I have business to finish, and I intend to leave at dawn for al-Qurnah." He paused for a moment then resumed: "I should prepare things for the journey and then get some sleep." He braced himself for an interrogation.

The uncle gazed into the eyes of Hameed as though to read the lad's thoughts. "You surprise me, son!" he said, glancing at his mates before fixing his eyes again on his nephew.

Hameed felt uneasy. As a scrupulously honest person, he hated to behave as a prevaricator, particularly towards his uncle. "Uncle … there is an urgent work task to finish there," he stressed, and then added with docility, "I will not be absent more than a couple of days."

Abū Hasna cast an unsatisfied look at Hameed, yet it was mixed with inherent kindness and care. Then he addressed Hameed, reminding him, "At dawn there will be no mator,"[29] while his own mind

---

[29] A *mator* is a large, motor-equipped boat that transfers people of the marshes to the small peripheric towns.

was wondering about what business was so urgent that his nephew must leave while Hasna was in such critical condition—especially after the revelation of the wondrous cure by Sayyid Majeed.

"Yes, Uncle, I know! For that reason, I'll go in my boat," Hameed anxiously replied while seized by fear that his uncle might suggest that he wait till midday to go by mator. Fortunately, abū Hasna didn't follow that path. Instead, he groaned softly, then after a steadfast look at his nephew, he turned his eyes to the other two men, who were watching and listening during this short interchange. Hameed too looked in that direction, and he was ruffled by the manner in which the clergyman furrowed his eyebrows and by his quizzical aspect, which communicated something akin to disbelief mixed with apathy, or at least that's what Hameed imagined.

Hameed wasted no time. He grabbed his megwar and rose to his feet while avoiding the trenchant, provoking look of Sayyid Majeed. Hameed took two short steps forward, bowed before the clergyman, and without looking into his eyes, kissed his right hand.[30] After that he shook hands with abū Jawda.

The uncle, who was already on his feet, saw his nephew to the door and there hugged him goodbye. "Take care, my son. I pray that you will come back safely."

Once outside, Hameed strode through the black of the moonless night. Soon the fierce barking of dogs, irritated by the solitary intruder, shattered the smooth silence.

---

[30] A social habit to show respect for the sada.

4

The next day, before twilight, Hameed commenced his voyage. The heaven was strewn with only the largest gleaming stars. The air was utterly still and heavy with an overhanging obnoxious smell. At such times, when all things were immersed in the silent void and soaked into a ghostly mist, solitude reigns and the marshes acquire the mystic chill of a haunted waterscape with a touch of hallucination. In that dark grey world, mythic imaginations were unleashed from their haven of the primordial human subconscious, and the legacy of epochs of superstition and metaphysical illusions unfolded itself, thus conjuring up extraordinary fancies of fearsome creatures prowling among the dense reeds, of shadowy forms floating on the waters, and of dripping fuzzy shapes appearing on the exposed pinnacles of submerged tells.[31] Yes, at dawn, these realms acquired a fabled, dreary, and horrifying aspect where fear could shake the bravest of hearts. Amid these creepy sensations, Hameed cast a look upon the sleeping village and then poled his boat away from the murky shoreline. The light vessel slithered through the quiet waters. He paused for a second or so to raise his head towards the sparsely dotted sky, took his bearings, and then steered his way towards the deep waters ahead in the northward direction, towards al-Dawaya, instead of the presumed eastward direction of al-Qurnah. When the boat drifted away from the peripheral shallow waters, the young man pulled the

---

[31] Tells are archaeological hills that represent sites of past Mesopotamian civilisation.

mardie out of the water, lined it along the length of the boat, and sat on the back deck to grip the oars. As he rowed ahead, the oars made a rhythmic sound which resembled that of clapping hands. Time slowly passed by. The dawn sky quietly laboured to deliver a new morning. On the eastern horizon, above a mixture of crimson hue and fading grey shade, the Morning Star appeared proud but with an ever dwindling brightness. Still higher in the sky, the heavenly canvas took on a hazy bluish tone that progressively swallowed the last of the night stars. On the earth, the reed expanses drew a wide continuous swath in the southern and western directions. In eastern and northern directions, the papyrus stems extended as discrete isles. The marsh vegetation appeared, under the infantile light of the new day, solid and impressive. It was not long before the first sunrays rose above the horizon and the world was gradually bathed in the transient purple shower of the early sunshine.

Hameed felt a refreshing sensation as a rare whiff of morning breeze stirred the dull air and touched his sweat-beaded face. When he turned his head around, he saw the dark line of the dense reeds far behind him. He let down the oars, rested his elbows on his knees, and looked thoughtfully at the scene before his eyes. A vast marsh, an uninterrupted water expanse, al-Barga, extended to the limits of human vision. The marsh surface was so still that it looked like a frozen water field. Hameed shaded his eyes with his right hand and glanced to the eastern sky. The sun was well above the horizon, and the glare from the falling golden rays grew uncomfortable. The young man surveyed the horizon. Then he bent forward to grip the oars and thought to himself, *There is a long way to go.* He paddled headlong towards his destination. To an observer, the young man would look impressively equipped. Two black leather bandoliers criss-crossed his chest, and a waist belt with a gun holster rested just below his right elbow. He also had a sheathed curved dagger attached to the waist belt. In front of him, at the bottom of the boat, there lay some other provisions: a medium-sized well-wrapped bundle, a spade, a *minjal*,[32] a *fala*,[33] a *qirba*,[34] and a long Brno rifle loosely wrapped in a pale blue rag. Indeed, had his companions of last night cast a look at him today, armed and equipped to the teeth, they would certainly think he had an evil, morbid purpose.

The world around Hameed, in contrast to his inner turmoil, was peaceful and serene. The pale green waters dazzled under the falling sunrays; the blue sky was empty and forsaken; and the retreating distant dark reeds lost their entity and appeared as a thin dark line. There was no sign of human activity except for a distant ascending white smoke column in the south-easterly direction. Hameed stopped paddling for a moment to roll up his long sleeves to just above the elbows, then he resumed rowing with his body swinging to and fro. Soon the slackened boat gained momentum once more and pulled away. The sun rose higher in the sky, and with that both the heat and the dampness escalated, rendering the atmosphere sluggish and unpleasant. The body of the lonely rower

---

[32] A *minjal* is a toothed sickle.

[33] A *fala* is a forked fishing spear.

[34] A *qirba* is a filled water skin.

was bathed in sweat. His black hair shimmered like obsidian beneath the falling sunrays. The blue sky had gradually lost its clarity as windblown sands from the bounding western and northern local deserts hung high in the sky and extended as dull streaks of dust, muddling the heavenly ceiling. This atmospheric turbidity is a sign declaring the approach of high noon.

Hameed felt an uncomfortable stinging in his eyes as sweat drops dripped into his eyeballs. He dropped the oars, untied the yashmagh from around his neck, and dried the profuse perspiration that wet his whole body. Then he looked ahead. The vast, featureless world showed absolute symmetry in all directions, exposing a tedious, discomforting monotony through which the young boatman worked his way relentlessly northward. Through the translucent veil of dust, the blurred sun was seen high and indistinct. Then, at a certain moment, Hameed sighted a dark hairline that he recognised as the mark of a remote vegetation zone. He knew it well. It was Hurat umm al-Khanazeer,[35] his destination. As he looked contemplatively towards that distant linear target, a fish jumped from somewhere and made a tiny splash, which broke the wall of silence and brought him a vivid sensation. After drying his face, he spat into his hands, rubbed them together, once more caught the oars, and steered forward.

The sun was well past the zenith when Hameed neared Hurat umm al-Khanazeer. The sun set the reeds ablaze with an intense yellow lustre. The full-grown

[35] Hurat umm al-Khanazeer literally means "the marsh of the pigs".

tall vegetation appeared formidable and impenetrable with a primitive and unyielding aspect. Indeed, this part of Hor al-Hammar's marshes had a notorious reputation. It was the most isolated part, a big island of sedges and rushes that was almost untrodden by humans. These circumstances rendered the place a closed habitat: a niche for wild pigs and a paradise for winter migrant birds that now had departed, leaving behind only a few native waterfowls. The scanty travellers who happened to pass at a distance from that desolated region gaped in ghastly awe at the view and hurriedly continued on their way to their respective destinations. The obnoxious physical milieu of Hurat umm al-Khanazeer inspired fearful tales and chilling hearsay. Many respectful persons in al-Chebayesh and al-Fohoud swore that this uninhabited location had become, particularly after sunset, the haven for Sa'alat and Tantal.[36] Unidentified witnesses swore that they had glimpsed, from a distance, these two terrifying creatures. In short, the locality had become the most hideous, the scariest, and the most macabre place in the whole marsh region.

The young man stopped rowing, and soon the boat came to a standstill. He faced the colossal silent scene with obscure apprehension. There was something fiendish and wicked about the whole setting of the sight. His mind unconsciously recalled all the dreary tales about this horrendous area, which cast upon him an ominous and repulsive feeling. It was only through

---

[36] Sa'alat (female) and Tantal (male) are two mythological creatures who torture their victims in terrible ways before devouring them.

the summoning of the purpose of his journey that he was able to fight back these ghastly feelings and endure the facing gloom. So, sidestepping the disturbing sensations, he tilted his head back a little bit and closely inspected the interwoven reeds, sedges, and rushes, searching for a path. In his immediate surroundings he didn't recognise a passage, so he rowed slowly around the irregular contour of reeds and kept a watchful eye as he went along. After rowing for some time, he beheld a location where the vegetation parted sufficiently for the boat to go through. He pulled the oars and laid them on the bottom of the boat. He grabbed the mardie and stood at the rear deck, then watchfully steered the mash-houf and toiled up the constricted path.

The atmosphere was quite heavy, and breathing was a painstaking effort. The towering vegetation kept pressing against the creeping boat from both sides, and Hameed could hardly make headway. During the slow movement, the young man suffered from the pricking of pointed reeds and the stings of spiky underbrush. The narrow, winding waterway resembled a semiclosed sewage tunnel. He hoped it would fan out soon somewhere ahead. The choking air was saturated with the unpleasant smell of the decayed things of this rotten wetland. It was a steamy, tight environment. He panted and breathed hard while his body became completely wet, which made him feel the burning sensation from the fresh raw scratches and cuts. The friction of the boat with the bordering plants made a hissing sound that frightened a waterbird in a concealed nest, which made the undergrowth rustle as the bird flew away with fluttering wings and a cry: "Kaka-kee, kaka-kee."

The narrow painful path continued for some distance before widening into a dark grey-brown pool. Hameed steered the mash-houf straight to the edge, and soon it ran aground on the muddy bottom. With heaving chest and pounding heart, the young man leant on the mardie. His face had the unmistakable look of both fatigue and thoughtfulness as his eyes roamed the surroundings. The encircling papyrus wall was a disconsolate scene. Hameed laid the mardie full length along the boat, got out of the boat, and with callused bare feet waded in the shallow, murky waters. The stagnant water was just above his ankles. With a couple of steps he reached a small muddy strip that was, for an unknown reason, free from vegetation, which afforded him a landing place. He turned around, put his arms akimbo, and examined once more the four corners of the site. Then he nodded, saying, "This is a suitable place." He sighed, knowing that it would take him more time and effort to find another, better location. He glanced up at the turbid sky as if to estimate the time of day, then he strode towards the boat and pulled it onto the muddy ground among the reeds. He stood up straight, facing the prolific vegetation, pulled up his dishdasha, and then relieved himself. The sun, with dull brightness, simmered the world, the still air rippling with intense heat. There was no shade and no shadow, and the sultry air was damp, transforming any activity into an arduous work.

With the intention of finishing his work before sunset, Hameed decided to take a brief break. He drew near the boat and stretched out his right hand to grab the pale blue rag bundle that was in the bottom of the mash-houf. He sat on the edge of the boat and cradled the bundle carefully in his lap. He unfastened the loose knot. Inside there were two smaller bundles. He chose one, the food bundle, and untied it. It was a meagre provision and a stodgy meal. There were pieces of thick, grey-blue rice bread (*tabag*), a few brown onions, and lumps of *khurrait*.[37] Using his clenched right fist, he smashed one onion head on the edge of the boat and started eating morsels of bread with the onion. The dry food obliged him to gulp water from the water skin, the qirba. As soon as he finished his hasty meal, he put the two bundles back into the boat and stood, ready to start his work. Lurking scary imaginations, the solitude, and the harsh atmosphere of the virgin location all put a painful strain on both his mind and body. Yet he had sufficient purpose and concentration on his mission to resist these adverse effects. In preparation for his activity, and to make his movement more comfortable, he raised the front hem of his dishdasha and clipped it onto his belt. Then he took the toothed sickle from the boat, squatted on the narrow, drenched strip, and started cutting the dense plants with alacrity. The scorching heat and stagnant air rendered the routine work exhausting, yet he worked agilely and in an effective manner. Once or twice he stopped briefly to blow his nose and to quench his thirst by quaffing water from the qirba, then resumed his work. He planned to make a shelter. For this purpose, the area provided but fragile resources: mud and reeds. Digging a pit or a trench was an easy task in this soft ground, but it was

---

[37] Khurrait is foodstuff unique to the people of the marshes. It is extracted from the yellow powdery material produced by the reed plants.

out of the question as the groundwater was almost level with the ground surface; one single stroke from the spade would be sufficient to cause water seepage. Therefore his plan was to clear enough area to collect sufficient mud and mix it with the reeds to make the material for constructing a low structure or shelter.

Clearing the spot took Hameed longer than he had expected. When it was accomplished, he raised to his feet, panting, and mopped his face and neck with the loose headcloth. He examined the cleared area and felt satisfaction, so he let the sickle drop to the ground and extended his right hand into the tobacco sack that was dangling from his waist belt. He picked one Bafra rolling paper, stuffed it with the brown-yellow stuff, and rolled a cigarette. Then he squatted, facing the pool, and ignited the cigarette with the lighter. He started smoking.

In that moment of transient inactivity, thoughts ran through his head. His mind wandered off to his village, to Hasna. He visualised how the glow of her wide, black eyes had grown dull to the extent of being extinguished, and with that an admixture of deep sadness, nostalgia, and anxiety seized him. But he couldn't stay in such a mood for long as the steamy atmosphere, the smelly pool, the grim monotonous foliage, and above all his mission checked his sentimental buoyancy and called him back to the critical task ahead. So, the influx of homebound thoughts slowed as soon as he finished his cigarette and rose to his feet. He threw the tiny cigarette butt into the pool, and with his thumb and index finger he removed a tobacco leaf stuck on the tip of his tongue.

Sombre but determined, Hameed strode towards

the boat and grabbed the spade. He walked away from the water's edge to the far end of the cleared space and started to collect mud by shallow-scooping and shovelling the water-soaked earth. The extracted dark, rich, organic mud steamed with a strong foetid odour, and the young man, with a sour expression on his face, panted heavily and gasped for air as he went on with his work. Heat, sweat, and dirt rendered his skin, as well as his matted hair, sticky, akin to the viscous soil he was digging in. His body and clothes were smeared with the dark mud. After an hour or so of exhausting labour, there was a large heap of mud. For the next step, Hameed started to collect and stack the cut reeds. He used the spade to chop the tubular stalks into smaller pieces. After that he mixed the short-cut vegetation with the soft earth. When he finished blending the two ingredients, he stopped for a while, sweltering. He used his sleeves to wipe his face, and then he Leant against the shaft of the spade, reflecting on the scene of his work amid the peculiar quietude of the surrounding milieu. It was a lethargic environment in which a deluge of lurid heat reigned. The only moving thing was the large, bluish biting flies that constantly disturbed him. This is why he felt company when he heard the distant quacking of a coot or the nearby chirping of a solitary grasshopper. He gazed with blinking eyes at the sky. The sun perceptibly descended. "I should finish my place to spend the night before the evening," he mumbled as he hurried to make a low circular rampart using the admixture. When he finished, there was a dark, stinking barricade of sufficient height for him to crouch within its confines.

Hameed went around the soft structure and used

his spade to make minor reparation strokes and to add reinforcement here and there. Then, finally, he let out a sigh of relief. However, there remained a small but necessary detail to attend to. Groundwater slowly oozed into the shelter. With his sickle, he stooped once more and started to cut more papyrus. He used his hands and knee to break the collected stalks and laid them evenly inside the circular shelter, thus making a loose mat flooring over the water-saturated ground. With this being done, he stood up. The dark blue mud covered his hands and surrounded his feet up to the ankles. He scraped his feet vigorously with the edge of the metal spade to get rid of the viscous material, after which he threw the spade aside. He bent to pick up a fresh rush stem, which he slashed open with his dagger, and ate its fresh pith while his eyes were looking at the blazing western sky.

The encircling soaring plants caused duskiness to settle long before the sun went below the horizon. The sky had already lost its turbidity and became clearer with the diminishing of the suspended dust and the cessation of sandstorms from the dry western flatlands. But the heat showed no abatement as the lower level of air of the enclosed space retained its stewing, intense heat and suffocating humidity. The long arduous labour and the environmental inconveniences had taken their toll on Hameed. And now with the physical work accomplished, he felt very hungry. He went to the boat and grabbed the food bundle, but he instantly felt a desire for a fresh meal. *The pool is teeming with fish,* he thought to himself. *I must hurry! The light is fading, and I have no lantern.* So, hurriedly he went to the boat to fetch the fala, the four-headed fishing spear. Once it was in hand, he waded into the pool. He strode deeper into the murky waters. Then he stopped and held the fishing spear in the air with his right hand and watched the water attentively. Before long, he got his opportunity and targeted a medium-size fish, which he impaled with one throw. It was a well-rounded *hemri*.[38] With the frantically flopping catch on the forked spear, Hameed retraced his steps towards the cleared patch, and once there, he freed the fish and caught the twitching, slippery body firmly by the left hand. Sitting on the edge of the boat facing the pool, he pulled out his dagger and slashed the fish open down the back, and then wiped the blade on his dress before putting it back into the sheath. He removed the entrails, threw them away in the pool, and put the slashed fish on the rear deck.

Light of the day was fading fast. Hameed collected the driest stalks from the remaining cut papyrus and made a campfire. The reeds burned slowly, and the vacillating flame lit up the rising thick white smoke. He picked up the fish from the boat and hung it upright on three pointed slashed reeds, which he had fixed in the muddy ground, with the cut side of the fish facing the fire. As dimness built up the air swarmed with mosquitoes and the smoke of the small fire, which ascended upward vertically with no lateral drift and helped but little to dissipate the stinging insects.

Now as he squatted, watching the fish roasting slowly, and having been released from physical work, his mind became more susceptible to the choking isolation and shadowy solitude of the location. The

---

[38] *Barbus luteus.*

falling darkness turned the encircling monotonous vegetation into a dispiriting scene, a solid vertical wall of consummate opacity. Facing that tenebrous wall, he found himself seized with alarm. He moved towards the boat, grabbed his rifle with one hand and the food bundle and the qirba of water with the other, and went back beside the fire. He sat cross-legged, with the long rifle across his lap. Hameed's eyes watched the grilled fish cooking slowly on the small fire, which gave off a delicious smell that ameliorated the horrible odour of the place. He poked his finger into the broiled meat and found it well-cooked and crispy, so he lifted the fish from the pointed reeds and laid it down on its back on the dying fire. He untied the food bundle and commenced eating his meal with voracity. He chewed and swallowed the morsels of his food quickly while his eyes moved around restlessly, scanning the impenetrable, abysmal obscurity.

The enclosing morose darkness made him feel terribly lonely. It also facilitated the darting of daunting thoughts and gruesome imaginations, which transferred the apparently slumberous place into a shadowy animated world. When he finished his meal, the fire became less radiant with subdued flames. So, he threw additional reeds onto the fire and blew on the flames with his mouth to revive the vigorousness of the fire, which soon went up in flames again. Hameed stood up and walked warily towards the pool, where he crouched on the brink of the water and used his right hand to scoop the dark mud. He started to smear his hands, feet, neck, and face with the viscous stinking slurry to shield the uncovered parts of his body from the tormenting stings of the tiny insects. Then, he straightened up and cast a pensive look towards the sky and his surroundings. There are two hemispheres to the enclosing nocturnal world: the higher, sky-bound glowing one and a lower, earthbound, impermeable one. The heavens sparkled with innumerable lurid stars. And across this August night sky, frequent falling stars cleaved the celestial dome, with streaks of fire behind them. In contrast, earth exhibited another, nonconvivial image. It was pitch-black, unwavering gloom saturated with a suspicious stillness—a cradle for the horrible tales that suddenly sprang, vividly, in the mind of the young man. In such an unpleasant, creepy setting where myths and solid reality merged and became one, where actual fears with auditory and visual components intermingled with invisible horror that mimicked morbid hallucinations and the icy breath of formless danger, the metamorphosis of this isolated, untrodden swampy realm into a consternating, haunted world was an appalling mental experience.

By now, the fire had gone out, and the place lay under the burden of pitch-darkness. Hameed, beset by ghostly fears and invaded by terrifying visualisations, reached for his rifle, tucked the small food bundle under his arm, grabbed the qirba, and with the aid of the spade handle hopped inside the circular barricade as though in search of safety against an impending threat. He put the bundle and the water skin on top of the low mud rampart and gazed anxiously around himself as though expecting something to come out of the heart of the opaque blackness. His bare feet rested on the loose mat of rushes and reeds that had become wet as a result of groundwater seepage. The stinky, unpleasant smell of the decayed organic matter filled his nostrils. It was quite repulsive, a nauseous odour that obliged him to wrap his headcloth around his nose and mouth. So, with a dusky countenance matching the darkness of the moonless night, he knelt on his knees, holding the long, heavy rifle, while his ears were attentive to the anxiety-provoking silence. In this static posture, he felt himself wearier and more exhausted than he was moments before. It was as if the fatigue of the day had suddenly set its complete load on his body. Physically he was on the verge of yielding to the enormous bodily stress, but the scary imaginations that invaded his mind kept him adequately vigilant.

He stared through the featureless blackness and felt but a vague, inscrutable disquietude. His stressed mind even made him hear imaginary frightful sounds. It was puzzling how an absolute silence could communicate the dreadful howling of beasts, the appalling clatter of hellish hoofs, and heart-chilling ghostly shrieks. It was a spooky world. The frightening impact of these auditory imaginations, as they lacked extrinsic aspect, assumed even more dreariness when they were supplemented by visual illusions, undoubtedly a symptom of his strained mind, which made him feels as though all the ghastly creatures of myth had been unleashed at that moment. It was an instant of hallucinatory seizure that was developing to the point of being excruciating.

Hameed squeezed his temples then shook his head vigorously as if to tear this web of misty fears asunder. Then he thought it might do him good to light a cigarette, so he lit one. As he exhaled the smoke of the cigarette, he started to mull over his purpose and associated plan. And with that the flood of nebulous sensations gradually decelerated and gave way to reason and rational thinking. He realised that he should keep his awareness alive and focus on menacing realities. "I must accomplish my mission," he murmured to himself, nibbling his bottom lip. Then with a sentimental shift in his thoughts he muttered to himself, "I wonder how Hasna is now. Is she awake? Maybe she is unconscious? Did they tell her about the revelation of Sayyid Majeed? If so, is she in better spirits? Is she more hopeful?" This series of wishful thoughts prompted him to envision, with nostalgic but saddening feelings, the glare of her wide black eyes dwindling into an extinguished look, begging for a glimpse of life. And with that he felt something traumatic deep down in his heart.

This emotional sailing helped him to mitigate the grip of morbid imaginations and brought him straight back to his purpose. O youth! What stunning, poignant convictions! For Hameed, his bond with Hasna was invulnerable to the tragic ways of destiny. His soul was charged with defiance and full of a confidence that was as strong as blind faith! Yet, every now and then a depressive, inscrutable thought appeared in his mind and his countenance changed, momentarily becoming sober and realistic. Thus, with fluctuating states of mind, he Leant his left elbow against the soft barricade while his chin rested on his right arm that held the rifle with the muzzle pointed towards nowhere, for in that ominous darkness he couldn't even see his fingertips, but he hearkened to the primordial silence with alertness and anticipation.

The irritating stillness continued for hours, during which he smoked and changed his posture several times. Towards midnight he heard, or he imagined hearing, feeble sounds; it seemed like the sound of breaking reed stalks, and that brought him to a state of heightened alert, but nothing followed. The drowsy quietness resumed its course, interspersed only by the buzzing of sleepless and whirring mosquitoes that were trying all the time to find an uncovered spot amid the mud insulation on his skin. "What an association—perilous silence and tiny biting devils!" he grumbled to himself, fidgeting a little as he felt stiffness in his back and joints. He stared at the facing opaqueness, and it stared back at him. Once or twice he felt a sort of giddiness. Gazing continuously through the sheer darkness was dizzying. It was like looking into an inscrutable void that enjoyed latent fullness which could manifest itself, horribly, at any moment. He was aware that if something were to come out of the thicket, he would neither be in position to recognise its identity nor be able to take the appropriate action. This realisation implied that staying on watch was ineffective and nonproductive for his purpose, that he had to wait for daylight.

So, his vigilance was not a totally intended measure; rather it was also an expression of his stress, his inability to relax. Yes, he was able to suppress, at times, the mythic fears, but his real anxieties were all the more demanding, which caused insomnia. It was one of his personal habits that stress incited him to eat voraciously. So, he extended his hand to grab the food bundle, from which he took a piece of rice bread and munched it tastelessly. At times he wondered how it was possible for such utter stillness to be a harbinger of what he expected to encounter. Hameed raised the qirba to his mouth to quench his thirst and gulped water, at which moment he caught the face of the sky.

The map of the night sky progressively changed. Constellations shifted westward, and new stars replaced others, garnishing the tenebrous firmament with an enchanting glow. The young man sighed. There was a saddening contrast between the festive serenity of the celestial realm and the repelling aspect of the surrounding earthly gloom. He had no knowledge of star names except for the polar star and Najm Suhail,[39] and the constellation Banat Na'ash, but he loved this remoteness that seemed to him beyond terrestrial suffering and the home of everlasting happiness. *In the sky there is no sickness, no suffering, no monsters,* he thought, then he added with a faint smile, *and no mosquitoes!* He thought how wonderful it would be that he and Hasna would be there!

But these flights of imagination didn't last long. Reality dragged him back to the actual miserable conditions that engulfed him. His body became increasingly strained, and his muscles cramped as a result of crouching for hours in that fetid place. Drowsiness invaded him several times, but he fought it back by lighting a cigarette. At about two o'clock in the morning, somnolence reigned and his alertness waned considerably. He couldn't keep his fruitless vigil any longer. Finally, the dominion of sleep overpowered his senses. His head fell on his stretched arm, and he slipped into a deep slumber.

---

[39] Najm Suhail is Canopus; Banat Na'ash is the Big Dipper.

5

It was starkly dark when Hameed suddenly woke up, or rather was awakened by a rustle, some sort of trampling on rushes and a low grunt. He feverishly clutched the rifle and assumed an aiming posture. His eyes frantically stared around, but it was too dim to see anything. His heart thudded heavily in his heaving chest. The deep silence amplified and trumpeted his pounding heartbeats. Anxious and uncertain, he Leant against the low mud barrier and listened attentively, but he could perceive nothing other than the nocturnal silence. With the persistence of this nothingness, he became unsure and hesitant; however, the situation reactivated the suppressed supernatural legacy. His mind once again became susceptible to ghostly imaginations and prey to disheartening tales. There was the creepy sensation that the darkness concealed an animated world, that it was full of latent horror and crowded with stealthy, invisible forms. With stressed body and tensed muscles, he turned his head, like a periscope, to each of the four directions as if suspecting the emergence of a sneaky devilish creature or the menace of a lurking abyssal monster. So, the mythos in him had popped out, yet—fortunately—it didn't last long. The logos brought him back to reality and to the grave challenges he was facing.

Paradoxically, the same elements that had activated his metaphysical fears, namely the sudden undefined sound that had awakened him, the gruesome milieu, and the bleak mouldy environment, incited him to rebel against these aphotic fears. "Man! Do not rave!" he rebuked himself. Now with rational thinking gained ground, his mind tackled what had awakened him in a different way. At first, he thought that it could have been a nightmare or an illusory effect induced by both fatigue and the muggy atmosphere. But soon afterwards he thought, *No, it wasn't a nightmare.* He irresolutely mumbled, "There is something real out there." He scratched his mud-covered skin and felt himself to be like all the decaying plants in this quagmire. Then he rose to his feet and held the rifle between his legs. He slid his hand into the tobacco sack and started to roll a cigarette. With a swift flick of the thumb, he ignited the lighter. The flame flared up with an intense glare in the heart of that tenebrous night, which made Hameed's eyes gleam like micaceous flake. He gripped the rifle in his left hand, with the butt resting on his bended knee, and started sucking on the cigarette tensely in rapid intervals, which made the tiny ember put forth a miniscule but distinct glimmer in the gloom. The exhaled smoke seeped through his mouth and nose and dissipated in the putrid air. He apprehensively faced the encamping murkiness, and soon wild, unstrained imaginations once again impinged upon his mind. "What an ill-fated spot! What a suspicious gloom!" he grumbled uneasily. "The devil might have a coterie of unseen disciples treading through the obscure depths!" But with his wobbling psychologic state, he flew in the face of these mythical imaginations. "I fear neither the devil nor his stealthy solders! Let them come!" he mumbled, crouching down.

Hameed was in a troubled sleep when he was awakened by a flutter and the melodious song of a solitary Basra reed warbler.[40] The sun was above the horizon, but it was still lurking behind the papyrus wall, which bestowed upon the tops of the high reeds a crimson hue. The young man, with pale face and weary aspect, rubbed his eyes and looked to the sky and to the overshadowing thick rushes. He was hungry, but he also felt an urge to relieve himself. He slung the rifle by its leather strap over his shoulder and used the spade to jump out of the shelter. He hurriedly walked towards the reeds, where he raised his dishdasha and squatted. After some time, he stood up and strolled towards the pool. He crouched and used both hands to scoop water to remove the mud layer that covered his body. There was much heat in the air even at this early hour of the day. As the young man was busy cleaning his body, his eyes cast a passing glance upon the narrow muddy strip at the far edge of the pool, to the right of the shelter, and he immediately felt a shudder run through him. He got to his feet, wiped his semiwashed hands on his dress, and unslung the rifle. Then, cautiously, he shuffled his feet forward. After a few steps, he stopped and stood stone-still. There were hoof prints in the viscous mud. And to his astonishment, the marks were oddly large and deep, which brought him a shiver. "So, it was not a bad dream but a reality," Hameed tremulously mumbled. The very fact that the creature was so close filled him with anxiety. *The beast is out there lurking in the dense rushes,* he thought worriedly. *It could come again anytime!* He was overwhelmed by apprehension as though the wild animal would make an imminent appearance.

---

[40] A bird known locally as "al-Ghareed al-Basrawi".

Reflexively he strode rapidly, almost trotting, to the shelter. He hunkered down inside the barricade, assuming a shooting position. The sunshine streamed above the vegetation wall. His eyes surveyed the space around him with tense expectation, but all that his senses revealed was the muteness of an almost static world. No flutter, no hissing, no buzzing, and no cracking of a single dry sedge. Even the surface of the pool was flat with no ripples. It was some sort of abstract, pure stillness that fills the soul with melancholy. Yet the young man had the paradoxical sensation that this deafening muteness had a specious aspect, a concealed latent clamour that could be unleashed at any moment.

Hameed's state of intense alertness lasted for quite some time, but the continuation of tranquillity around him caused his watchfulness to gradually ebb. And with that his initial feeling of hunger bit him again. He grabbed the food bundle and opened the loose knot. As was his habit when he was stressed, he quickly gobbled the dry food. Then he drank some water and knotted the food bundle again. Then he pondered the situation. He was particularly worried by the unusual dimensions of the hoof prints. There was a need to inspect the animal tracks more thoroughly, so he rose to his feet and left the rampart.

Holding the rifle in both hands, he made a cautious advance to the location and crouched beside the hoof prints. "It is a wild boar," he concluded after a while. There were two intermingled but opposing hoof tracks between the pool and the dense vegetation. Hameed stood up and moved towards the wall of reeds. There he saw traces through the dense tubular plants, a tunnel-shaped trail denoting the passage of the animal.

The way the tubular stalks were trampled down spoke of quite a massive animal. "The brute crushed every stem in its path," he said. Before discovering the traces on the soft mud, Hameed's anxiety had had a mostly abstract, shadowy, mythical nature. But now it assumed physical incarnation. In face of the lurking foe, he evoked his mission, which elicited his doughtiness, so he firmly clutched his weapon and mumbled, "I'll get him!" Then he retreated in rapid steps to his shelter.

The sun rose up in the sky, and with that the bright blue celestial disk gradually grew turbid with the commencement of western dust storms that blew up from the Afak desert. The air exhaled a simmering heat, and the dark wet ground breathed out a foul odour. The atmosphere teemed with blue-green biting flies that replaced the mosquito armies of the evening. As the day progressed, Hameed, terribly stinking with sweat streaming down his sticky skin, remained on watch while entrenching himself in the sickening hiding place. He stood, crouched and Leant with an ever-swinging mood as hope and fear tided and ebbed randomly. He ate, drank, smoked, fidgeted in place, urinated, scratched his body, and constantly dried his sweating face. And each time he used the headcloth, his black hair gleamed like waxed ebony. "I will decay in this rotten hole!" he grumbled as his resentment peaked at times. Apart from the buzzing of the flies and the occasional sound of a fish splashing or a teal quacking, silence reigned. Time passed by heavily. At high noon, the heat had accumulated to such an extent that the spot became like an infernal furnace. The water-laden soil steamed and radiated dizzying, invisible vapours that made breathing slow and laborious. It was a smothering environment characterised by extremes and excessiveness. The young man was almost at the end of his tether. The obnoxious conditions remained overly challenging, and Hameed's tense waiting was fruitless until a little before sunset.

As the sun dived behind the tall reeds and the low western sky kindled with an admixture of orange and red colours, at that short time of transition between day and night, things drastically evolved. Hameed was in the hideout eating a piece of khurrait when he heard rustling among the rushes on his right side. Unnerved and agitated, he let go of the food bundle and held the rifle in both hands. He lowered his head and looked over the top of the rampart in the direction from which the sound came. It was the very clear and unmistakable sound of movement shifting among the reed thicket. The sound was that of something treading on and brushing against the vegetation. His heart thudded strongly and his hands clutched the rifle tightly when he heard strong grunting. Then the dense plants swayed to disclose the moving creature. The young man was taken aback by what he saw. He stared and stared breathlessly into the face of what looked like an absolute horror, a physique of brute savagery that mirrored a menacing doom. He had never seen such a hideous and gruesome wild boar. It was enormously big with grey, stiff hair radiating from its thick skin like the bristles of a steel brush. The protruding crooked tusks were dull white and fearfully long. The young man stared, transfixed and unnerved by this sight of a primordial creature of terror. He could have voiced his astonishment, but his voice, fortunately, choked in his throat. *My goodness, what a beast!* he thought, feeling his heart turn within him while cold sweat dripped from his forehead.

For a fleeting moment he sensed a touch of doubt: the adversary seemed too herculean to overcome. Then almost immediately he overcame that disheartening feeling. *This creature will not win the battle!* he promised with an air of obstinate pride. The animal, unaware of the concealed man, emerged from among the entangled papyrus and slowly moved towards the pool. With barely the muzzle of his Brno rifle appearing above the rampart, Hameed jerked back the heavy bolt handle and then pushed it forward in four successive and fast movements, which inevitably produced a metallic ticking that didn't escape the sharp hearing of the wild boar. Being alerted, the animal first came to a standstill. Then it turned, as one single mass, to face the rampart. Hameed knew he must act fast. He had to take advantage of this short-lived stationary position of the animal. He aimed the muzzle at the target, took a deep breath, and uttered, "Bismillah!"[41] as he pressed the trigger. The sharp sound of rifle fire echoed like a rattling explosion. The bullet hit the huge body somewhere as the savage foe bellowed terribly and fiercely charged. Hameed, immediately after the first shot, raised his rifle again, retracted the bolt handle, pushed it again, realigned his sight, and aimed at the speedily approaching monster. There were the quick, heavy thuds of the accelerating hoof beats. The animal, rushing with astonishing momentum akin to that of a locomotive, had already come astride the mud barrier

---

[41] "In the name of God" This is spontaneous etiquette said as a good omen when starting work or an action.

when Hameed pressed the trigger and shot the second bullet before he was forced to stagger backwards as the massive animal fell on him. The bodies of the two foes collided violently with ensuing horrible clamour, a mixture of savage grunt and human scream manifesting the collision of two powers.

6

The world was in semidarkness. Peaceful serenity shrouded the village of Haj Raisan as dawn delicately embraced the sleepy marshlands. The tiny stellar lights gradually faded and disappeared, except for the more brilliant ones that shone faintly in the distance. All livings things, animals and humans alike, were in a deep sleep. Even the early risers, the cocks, were still in slumber. Yet there was one wide-awake soul, Hasna, following the prescription of Sayyid Majeed. It was the second dawn during which the girl had struggled hard to keep her eyes open, to remain in tormenting vigilance while waiting for the apparition of the wali, the portent of her cure. The two kerosene lanterns had been blown out but her mother, who slept nearby, alone after the departure of Zaira Tiswahen the day before, who had left a bottle of oil lamp on the floor. The ignited kerosene-saturated wick tip, which jutted out from dark date dough, put forth a vibrating sooty flame that tenuously lit the girl's ghostly face. In her semiconscious state, Hasna had rare brief moments of cloudy self-musing. She thought of her current languid existence, of the surrounding bleary world, and of her fragility and blatant physical vulnerability. She was saddened by how the picturesque world had become a prosaic realm devoid of pleasures and dreams, and by the fact that she was so emotionally drained. All this caused despair and passivity to evolve within her. However, the weird and prodigious revelation of Sayyid Majeed morally revived her and kindled the torch of hope. Like other people in her society, she had a strong belief in miracles. So, this raised her waning spirits and gave her the impetus to submit to the demanding requirement to stay awake and wait.

Hasna was partially lying on her side with her upper body reclined on two stacked pillows. She struggled hard to maintain her vigilance. She stared, with faint but hopeful eyes, through the circular window and watched the fading dimness. Her half-opened eyes surveyed the outside grey, auroral world that was perfectly still. The abstraction and obscurity of the revelation combined to her wishful thoughts stirred in her an ambiguous, psychic sensation that there was something in the air, some kind of feeble, imperceptible forerunner of a grand event. During her battle to stay awake, she dozed off several times. At one of these dozy instances she thought herself in a dream in which she first heard feeble sounds, a sort of faint splash followed by a hazy sight of solitary boatman who languidly appeared, thanks to his clear white dress, above the dark water, poling from a standing position. She made further effort and raised her head: "Is it a dream? A visual deception? Or maybe a figment of imagination?" the girl wondered as her eyes flung wide open in amazement. She exerted all what she had of energy to raise her frail body a little more and leant on her left elbow. She extended her free hand to clutch the rough frame of the rounded window and laboriously moved her face closer to the gap and stared again. It was real! What she observed was sheer vivid reality! And that immensely thrilled her. Her inner self was agitated and thrown into turmoil, but her carnal reaction, paradoxically, was negligible, almost null. She seemed mesmerised. No muscle flinched, and no word was uttered. There was a build-up of energy inside her, but it remained latent with no palpable somatic manifestation. Her eyes were moist as she watched the incredible scene.

The boatman had an actually unsteady pose with a slouched and somewhat crooked posture as he Leant heavily on the rowing pole, but these minutiae didn't capture the attention of Hasna, who was obsessed with the astounding miraculous appearance. The boatman was in a stark white dress, including his head and most of his face, which were covered by a white *ghutra*[42] that yielded a wondrous effect in the twilight. And down at his feet there lay a heaped mass of huge bulk. "Ah! The slain boar!" Hasna sighed hypnotically, and with that her eyes acquired a queer lustre as she arrived at the staggering recognition: the boatman was the wali! The sacred one, her saviour, was verily before her eyes! The anomalous apparition first engulfed the entranced girl in a numinous awe. Then it swept her into a rapturous delirium, which echoed in a shudder that passed through her body. The astounding scene kept her voiceless. During that short lapse of time, the wali passed by and moved a distance away to finally move his boat around the opposite patch of high reeds.

---

[42] A man's headcloth.

At that very moment the girl gasped for breath and heaved a deep sigh. Then she burst into tears and simultaneously let out an ear-splitting scream. At that moment her mother was sound asleep. The sudden scream woke her up; she was aghast, horrified and disconcerted. Her initial thought was that the fever had taken its toll on the brain of her daughter. She jumped from her bed and threw herself on the trembling girl, who was shaking like a leaf. "What is the matter, Daughter? What happened?" the bewildered mother enquired in a tremulous voice.

Concurrently, Hasna's father, awakened and alarmed, trotted towards his wife and daughter and frantically asked, "What is going on? What is there?"

The girl Leant her head against the frame of the circular window. She couldn't manage her thoughts as there was a gush of a multitude of emotions that whirled into her mind without her being able to translate them into meaningful words. The mother, after her initial guess, became mystified and uncertain about what had happened to her daughter. She gently pulled Hasna away from the window and strongly hugged her, feeling the strong pounding of the young heart. "Be quiet, Daughter, be quiet. ... What is there? Tell me, please!" the mother pleaded in a heartbreaking tone.

Hasna felt the anxiety of her parents. She partially turned her head around, and her woeful mother was amazed at the remarkable change that had fallen across the features of her daughter: the pallor of her face had acquired some vividness, her eyes were less dormant, and there was even a touch of rapture that floated over her visage. Now, as Hasna faced the bewildered, enquiring eyes of her mother, she first fell into a state of neurotic laughter while tears rained down her face. Then she uttered in a quavering voice, "Mother! Mother! I saw him! He is there!" With feeble, trembling hands, she incited her mother to look from the small window.

The mother, bedazzled and perplexed, moved her head near the opening and looked out apprehensively. The dull scene was mostly empty, except for the still water expanse and the opposite grey reed wall. The screaming of the girl, which had awakened her, made the mother first to think that Hasna was raving. But now her own wishful expectancy flashed in her mind the great hope they were all awaiting. "Whom did you see? Who was there?" the mother urged with great anticipation.

She craved to hear from her daughter but one thing. Therefore she was not completely caught off guard when the excited daughter elatedly cried, "The wali, Mother! I saw the wali!" The girl ecstatically rejoiced and drew a breath. "I saw him right before my eyes, in the boat; he was all in white, and the slain boar was at his feet!"

The mother was thrilled. What Hasna described was an exact transcript of Sayyid Majeed's divine remedy. For a fraction of a second, she gaped in wonderment, in tumultuous silence, at her daughter. Then she gasped. A miracle had occurred! And with that realisation, she felt all her grief and despair, which had encamped upon her heart for weeks, suddenly vanish. However, that mute stupor lasted but an instant, for the mother immediately, after that spellbinding moment, became galvanised, her heart brimming over with exhilaration. She felt the irresistible urge to herald this astounding happening to the world and to call everyone to share this eccentric moment. She raised her head a little, cupped one hand around her mouth, and uttered a long *halhoula*[43] that sharply penetrated the still dawn.

At that moment the father was still crouching beside his wife; he had listened to every word uttered by his daughter. On hearing the sharp trill, his accumulating excitement attained its highest level. So, with astonishing gaiety, he jumped and hurried to the other quarter of the dwelling, where he picked up his rifle, and strolled towards the entrance. He moved the rusty latch, opened the door, and rushed outside. Once he was in the open air, a frenzy gripped him. He raised the rifle high above his head and fired several discrete shots. The sound of the halhoula and the rattle of rifle shots terribly shook the sleeping village. Every living soul, humans and animals alike, had been agitated. The excited dogs fiercely howled; men seized their weapons and rushed outdoors, unnerved, astounded, and even frightened; and women and children followed on their heels. It was a scene of sheer hugger-mugger. The truth of the matter is that the perturbed people recognised, whether by way of physical indicators or by instinct, the source of the shocking sounds and hurriedly made their way, amid the uproar and clamour that was increasingly building all over Haj Raisan village, towards the hut of abū Hasna.

The first person who arrived there was the immediate neighbour, abū Jawda. He came running, barefooted and bareheaded. He raised his long

---

[43] A *halhoula* is a trilling cry of joy uttered by women during happy occasions.

dishdasha up to his knees with one hand and held his rifle in the other. "Haihum![44] Haihum, abū Hasna!" he shouted, his face betraying an unharnessed flurry of feelings. Abū Hasna, with swaying body and nested emotions, watched the multitude of men, women, children, and barking dogs encroaching upon him from all directions. The scene and the ever-growing tumult escalated his feverish state and threw him into another fit of vigorous emotionalism. He raised his rifle and fired another round of bullets. At that instant, abū Jawda stood directly in front of abū Hasna and enquired in a breathless voice, "Haihum, abū Hasna, what is there?"

The hysterical father, unable to contain himself any longer, slung the rifle over his shoulder, stretched both hands towards the stunned neighbour, caught him by the shoulders, and shook him passionately. "Dear abū Jawda! This is a blessed and cheerful morning!" When these words were uttered, a number of gasping men had already encircled the two. "The miracle happened, the apparition! Hasna saw the wali! She is saved," the excited father declared in a roaring voice as he looked triumphantly to the ring of people that was rapidly growing. The successive assertions were too fabulous and too enchanting to hear without being entranced.

Dumbfounded by what was declared, everyone in the crowd was speechless, but their silence didn't last more than a fraction of a second as suddenly someone among the multitude shouted wildly, "The wali appeared! The wali appeared!" The word *wali*,

---

[44] *Haihum* literally means "salute". It is usually used to signify support and backing.

with its massive connotation of sacredness and mysticism, had a tremendous electrifying impact on the crowd and caused a loud commotion. The people, with awe and enthrallment, immediately realised that something prodigious had occurred in their village, something akin to a divine incarnation taking place at this time and in this space. Therefore, the public frenzy that ensued was beyond mere emotional reaction. What actually happened was a mass shudder of hysterics. The individual vortices of irritation among the crowd, with an irrational vigour and primordial essence, intertwined with and converged into mass turmoil. A disharmonic, deafening uproar rose to the skies. The shouts of men, the piercing halhoulas of women, and the cries of frightened children conflated with the multitude of rifle shots, the barking of dogs, the bellowing of water buffalo, and the crowing of cockerels. The women, overwhelmed by wonderment and curiosity, turbulently poured into the small dwelling to have a look at Hasna and hear the details of what she had seen.

Soon the small place became unbearably overcrowded by the noisy incomers. Many were spewed out. The men, in large numbers, remained outside the entrance for some time, then they moved in a disorderly fashion to the mudhif, the spacious village guest house, which was soon choked by occupants. The surplus was forced to stay in the surrounding open space. By every measure it seemed an extraordinary morning. Every person was feeling that a bizarre, sacred air shrouded and blessed the village. The impact of the event assumed a tremendous tempo, and the village writhed in agitation, which made everyone think that the tapestry of land and sky had become different, that a divine touch had honoured their village. However, beyond the scene of the entranced inhabitants of Haj Raisan village, nature appeared aloof and apart, habitually running its course beyond human emotions and concerns.

7

The news of the spectacular event rapidly spread to all the villages of the marshes. The population, from Suq al-Shiyokh to al-Dawaya and from al-Fohoud to al-Mdaina, but also other villages farther inland, reacted with unprecedented convulsions as the weird event stirred vigorously the inherited sacred beliefs. The telling and retelling of what had happened produced, inevitably, further retouches, and the occurrence burgeoned into even more bewildering versions that triggered extra perturbation and excitement. Soon, people from nearby and distant villages were streaming in, in their boats, to set foot on the spot that was the focus of the phenomenon that had changed the rhythm of everyday life in Haj Raisan village. Lively activity replaced monotonous idleness, and exciting festivity substituted the tedious routine. An onlooker would observe that many single-coloured flags, in black, green, and red, had been raised atop the clumsy dwellings. Towards sunset, numerous fireplaces had been prepared, on which large, soot-smeared cooking pots, *qazans*, were set to prepare food for the crowds. A large number of volunteers who sought divine reward worked in the cooking and distribution of the speciality food *mfattah*[45] on large trays. High-ranking members of the society, such as chieftains, sada, and *serkals*,[46] as well as hajis[47] and the elderly, were served inside the ample mudhif. Those who had no place in the guest house were seated and served outside in the open air, where long, parallel rows of sedge mats had been spread on the ground. The mudhif looked grand and elegant with its cylindrical reedy arches, pillars, and criss-crossed high walls. The ground along the perimeter of the mudhif was covered with split-reed mats and date palm leaf rugs. Also supplied were soft wool rugs and pillows for the comfort of the guests. Right at the rear end of the mudhif, a black-skinned man sat on his haunches and was busy roasting the coffee beans on a fireplace. Then he grinded them in a large, heavy brass mortar to finally prepare the coffee in the many brass pots of different sizes which were halfway tainted with black soot, resting on a bed of glowing embers that yielded the slowly brewing coffee.

When the dimness of the evening set, numerous kerosene lanterns and mantle lamps were hung on the walls, along with three very brilliant pressurised kerosene lanterns set on the ground. Outside the mudhif, the space was lively and animated. The smell of burned dry dung, cooked rice, and cooked meat mixed with the foul, sulphurous smell of the marsh waters.

---

[45] Mfattah is cooked rice topped with large hunks of stewed meat and greasy dull white pieces of tail fat called *allyah*.

[46] The *serkal* is the deputy of the chieftain. Apparently, the word is modified from the Persian word *serkar*.

[47] *Hajis* is the plural of *haji*, which is a title given to a person who has performed a pilgrimage to Mecca.

The raucous atmosphere of the village continued for three consecutive days, during which Sayyid Majeed and Hasna were the two poles of attraction and great attention. While the girl became the focus of feverish curiosity as she was the subject of the remarkable event, Sayyid Majeed, on the other hand, was considered the spiritual mediator and revealer of the godly remedy. The fruition of the esoteric prescription lent undeniable credence to his knowledge of arcane matters and sacred truths that were beyond the reach of ordinary human beings. The bewildered people who swarmed the lofty guest house hurried to kiss the hands of the clergyman and rub their faces on his perfumed abaya to gain a blessing and benediction. In face of that hail of exaltation, the stout man pretended to keep a sober appearance, but his visage betrayed, to the keen observer, an unmistakable snobbery, elation, and pride at its highest level. It was a pitiable and miserable scene with these poor toilers rushing to kiss the hands of Sayyid Majeed, who every so often, and with a pretence of humbleness, withdrew his hands halfway—a theatrical movement that obliged the excited people to bow even lower to lay their dry, fissured lips upon the plump, soft hands.

The house of abū Hasna was the second place of gathering. It was where the women assembled. It acquired the air of a pilgrimage shrine and the gravity of a consecrated site. The women, motivated by the singularity of the event and guided by their inquisitive nature, were very keen to hear directly from Hasna. Inside the house, there was the noise of the mixed voices of women and crying babies. The limited space was saturated with the odour of incense, feminine perfumes, and body odour. According to social habits, upon entering the dwelling, a woman would utter a sharp halhoula and then spray *mlabbas*[48] in the air before dashing towards Hasna. In the beginning, the girl was enthusiastic to share her unique experience with other women, but repetition and redundancy started to draw heavily on her, and she found herself exhausted and unable to respond to the recurrent enquiries. Her mother was aware of the negative impact of this social pressure upon her daughter and decided to keep Hasna isolated from the growing crowd of women, so with the help of an elderly neighbour she cleared the inner room of visitors and gave herself the task of answering all enquiries in the raba'a. Furthermore, the insufficiency of the space to accommodate the ever-increasing comers made it necessary to have another reception place. The family of neighbour abū Jawda generously, opened their door for that purpose.

The visitors often did not come empty-handed. Most of them brought generous vow offerings and gifts such as sheep, hens, eggs, rice, and wheat flour. The pale-faced Hasawiyah[49] from the inland villages brought with them various vegetable products that they exclusively cultivated like tomatoes, green beans, cucumbers, and melons. The few weavers from nearby and distant villages came along with coloured, striped flat mats. These offerings were distributed between the

---

[48] Mixed sweets.

[49] Hasawiyah is a name given to the peasants who cultivate vegetables. Ironically, in spite of their productive life, they have a lower social status, an unfortunate fate they shared with another active group of villagers, the weavers.

family of abū Hasna and Sayyid Majeed. Food offerings, mostly vegetables, cooking oil, and rice, were mostly used and consumed in the preparation of the extensive public meals during the three days of festivity. Many people stayed in the mudhif till midnight indulging in long, fabulous tales and anecdotes while the host, abū Hasna, assisted by a few youths, had to stay to attend to the last guest and wouldn't leave until there was no need to serve anyone. The tradition is that the host is the last person who leaves.

After midnight, the mudhif did not remain empty. A few guests from remote villages had to spend the night and then depart the next day. So before leaving for his house, abū Hasna checked that everything was in order for the comfort of those who were spending the night in the guest house. Needless to say, the three ceremonial days were heavy, particularly on the part of abū Hasna's family, but even so, they were happy to serve the multitude who came forth to share with them the euphoria of the unique event which would be always remembered and deemed sacred. During these days of grand celebration, most of the attention of abū Hasna was directed towards serving the influx of people. However, at sporadic moments, a lurking worrying issue, an inkling of anxiety, flickered latently in his mind and momentarily disturbed his jovial mood. It was some sort of annoying thought that scintillated through his head like a distant, soundless flash of lightning. At such discrete instances he asked himself, *Where is Hameed? Why hasn't he come back yet?* But before he could go further into these vexing questions, he would be swept up again by the immediate urgent tasks that needed to be completed in the crowded guest house.

At midnight of the third day, the formal festivities came to an end. Guests from other villages had already left that afternoon. And though people gradually returned to the routines of everyday life, the awesome and wondrous sensation that a miracle had happened in the village of Haj Raisan remained with them. However, with the ebbing of the public ceremonial atmosphere and the dissipation of the many social obligations that had occupied almost all the time and energy of abū Hasna, the question of the absence of Hameed recurred now in his mind in a persistent, vigorous, and alarming manner. In the middle of the morning of the day following the festivities, abū Hasna crouched, poking the tiny embers beneath the coffee pot. He did not feel easy in his mind. Hasna was sleeping peacefully on a clean, ornamented mattress. His wife was nearby churning the milk by jerking the filled skin churn back and forth. From somewhere there came a birdsong. Abū Hasna looked up at the ceiling and saw an *alwiya*[50] calling to its chick in the nest. Except for that and the monotonous sound of the churning, stillness prevailed, which deepened his immersion into his own thoughts. For abū Hasna, the issue of his nephew became a matter of emergency as he could find no explanation for his nonappearance. Of course, he had strong reason to worry. Since Hasna had fallen ill, Hameed remained nearby, in the village. He

---

[50] *Alwiya* or *sinono* is the local name for a swallow. In the marshlands, people regard this bird with superstitious awe. They never disturb it in fear of an adverse fortune. This is why the bird lives peacefully and builds its nests on the ceilings of dwellings. The name also indicates the numinous hallow surrounding this bird.

had even told his uncle that he would not be away very long with his fiancée in that condition. So abū Hasna had every reason to wonder what could be keeping him away. "Now it is the sixth day since he left," abū Hasna murmured with a sombre, brooding expression on his face. "This is hard to digest." He did not wish to expose his solicitous thoughts to his wife, yet she easily recognised the signs of uneasiness in his aspect.

"What is the matter, abū Hasna?" she asked, shaking the skin churn.

The husband kept silent and did not reply. He was not sure whether his worries were justifiable enough to communicate them to his wife. He was careful not to spoil the phenomenal atmosphere that cloaked them all; instead, he resolved to utter a few reassuring words: "Nothing in particular. I just feel exhausted," he said in an evasive tone, and retreated into silence.

But what abū Hasna couldn't guess was that similar concerns about Hameed had been also circling in the mind of his wife. However, unlike her husband, her feminine propensity urged her to think aloud and release what was in her mind. She stealthily looked in the direction of her daughter to ascertain if she was asleep, then she spoke in low voice, "Zair, I am thinking of Hameed. Don't you think he should have been back by now?"

She bowed her head slightly to look into the neck of the churn and check the accumulating butter. Because of this, she missed seeing her husband when he impulsively raised his forefinger to the front of his mouth, but she did hear him say, "Hush!"

The woman raised her head again and resumed in a low voice, "I would have loved it if he were among us when that spectacular event happened." Then she vigorously blew into the churn, tied its neck, and resumed the rolling back and forth.

The talk of his wife affected abū Hasna in an odd way. He regarded this coincidence of worries as an evil omen, and this weighed further on his mind. He had a belief in the coupling of joy and sadness—a laughing mouth delivers a weeping eye. He looked at his wife and nodded. "I wished too he'd been here," he said elusively, and fell silent.

They both stopped speaking, and the muffled sound of churning filled the silence. Shortly afterwards, there was a knocking on the tin entrance door, followed by sound of clearing throat. The mother, anticipating the entry of a guest, rose to her feet, holding the churn with both hands, and moved to sit in the inner quarter. Abū Hasna rose to his feet and pulled down the pale cloth partition that separated the raba'a from the women's quarters, then he went to welcome his neighbour abū Jawda, who was waiting outside, and invite him in. The neighbour, with plain aspect, was still in the festive mood of the previous three days. He sat on the striped rug near the small hearth and smiled, apparently unaware of the stifled sombreness of his host. Abū Hasna served his neighbour heavy coffee in a small ornamented china cup and sat next to him, shoulder to shoulder. Then, with his head bent down, he spoke in a whisper: "Abū Jawda, I heard that Zair Saihoud will leave today to go to al-Mdaina and from there on to al-Qurnah. Is that right?"

His companion nodded in response. "Yes, he leaves around midday and will be back tomorrow or the day after tomorrow," he said, gulping his coffee down and casting a questioning glance at abū Hasna.

Abū Hasna hurried to raise the sooty pot. He poured more coffee into the empty cup that dangled from the hand of his neighbour. "Do you need something from Zair Saihoud?" enquired abū Jawda.

For a few moments the host appeared indecisive and remained silent. His restless eyes fell on the artless appearance of his companion, which, after all these long years of being neighbours, still captured his attention. He felt a need to speak his mind to his mate. He drew his head near to that of abū Jawda and spoke at length in a low voice, "I have worries, abū Jawda." He paused for a moment. "These might be gratuitous worries, I don't know, but I can't simply shrug them off."

The neighbour looked imperceptive of what he had heard and so he kept his relaxed, featureless countenance, which provoked the host to hurry and expose his core concerns. "Look, abū Jawda, six days have passed and still Hameed has not shown up!" He sighed, then his lips contorted. He added emphatically in a low voice, "You know, he left when we were in great distress. Doesn't that in and of itself make his absence for all these days seem odd?"

His companion slapped his wrinkled forehead and looked at him for a long time with his eyes wide open as if in wonderment that he had missed such a thing. Then he rushed to say in a high tone, "Yes, yo—"

But abū Hasna hastened to interrupt him in a whispering tone, "Hush! Don't raise your voice! I do not want umm Hasna to hear what we are talking about!"

With raised eyebrows, abū Jawda instantaneously attuned his voice with that of abū Hasna and said, reprimanding himself, "You are right. What obliviousness on my part! Hameed had not entered my mind once in all these days!"

Abū Hasna bent his head and dived once more into silence, but abū Jawda, with awakened curiosity, enquired, "What are you going to do now?"

The host looked at his neighbour while his mind was weighing an idea. Then he resolutely said, "Look, I am expecting more guests to come from Sayyid Dekheel and al-Nahia. I have to stay home these days." He paused, then added, "As you told me, Zair Saihoud goes to al-Qurnah today. I'll ask him to enquire and bring news about Hameed."

His companion nodded in agreement. "Yes, that would be the right thing to do."

Later, abū Hasna hurried to meet Zair Saihoud, a pale-faced, lanky elderly man who Leant on a crutch to steady himself. He was a trustworthy man who was not one to fall behind in his obligations. Abū Hasna asked him, without elaboration of the worries that he harboured in his mind, to meet Hameed, tell him about the fruition of the marvellous cure, and mention that his uncle wished him to come back immediately. Zair Saihoud assured abū Hasna that he would certainly do that. So with this arrangement, abū Hasna left for his home and spent the rest of the day and the early evening welcoming and serving a few visitors.

Before sunset of the next day, Zair Saihoud came back to the village. Without delay abū Hasna went, with combined apprehension and hope, to meet him. It was dim inside the house of Zair Saihoud as no lantern had been ignited yet. The man, who has just finished his prayers and was folding the soft prayer mat, showed an amiable face, took two steps towards abū Hasna, and invited him, in a somewhat high-pitched voice because he was hard of hearing, to sit on a newly woven braided rug. Stressed and full of anticipation, abū Hasna sat down. After serving his visitor a cup of coffee, Zair Saihoud addressed the issue directly. He told his visitor that he had gotten no news about Hameed. "Nobody has seen him in al-Qurnah. I asked many people, but no one has encountered him since his last visit two months ago," he said, noticing the misery unfolding on the face of abū Hasna.

"Have you asked at Atwan cafe? Or at the grocery of abū Adnan?" abū Hasna asked with a tremor in his voice. "Maybe some news is at the textile market?" he added in painful, wistful tone.

Zair Saihoud, with a feeble left ear, had already turned his head so as to hear him better. On capturing the pleading voice, he suddenly became aware of the amount of anxiety and disquietude of his friend. With that realisation he wished he could have brought him comforting news other than what he was telling him; but alas, there was no calming information. "My two nephews, Jassim and Flayeh, whom you know well, and I asked at these places and at others as well. No one has seen Hameed recently," he concluded with a shade of regretfulness on his face.

There was an instance of silence, and Zair Saihoud tried to fill in the gap by pursuing an alternate line of reasoning. "Are you sure he went to al-Qurnah? Could he be somewhere else?" He moved to light the lantern as he said this.

"No, he went to al-Qurnah," abū Hasna said in a voice lacking in energy, which obliged Zair Saihoud to crane his neck to hear him better. "He told me of his destination when he left six days ago. Both Sayyid Majeed and abū Jawda were present when he told me about his journey." That was a strong confirmation, which left Zair Saihoud looking at his mate mutely.

As a host and a friend, Zair Saihoud did his duty to lessen the irritation of abū Hasna by telling him there were no serious reasons to worry, that Hameed could have changed his mind and travelled to another destination. He uttered these calming words and followed them with litanies and short Koranic verses while his fingers moved up and down the beads of his black misbaha. But these carefully crafted words and verses did not soothe abū Hasna. Neither were they able to mitigate the angst that had befallen the man. The disappointment was beyond mitigation. Abū Hasna, with shaking hands, rolled a cigarette and lit it. Then he drew heavily on it and blew the smoke vigorously. Zair Saihoud was still mumbling litanies and holy verses. There was a lack of verbal exchange, so abū Hasna, with thwarted spirits and vacillating thoughts, made up his mind to leave as this visit had exhausted its purpose. His lips parted, and words followed in a strained high pitch: "Excuse me, Zair, I've got to leave." He put out the half-finished cigarette on the dusty ground. He rose to his feet, swayed a little, then balanced himself and shook hands with his host, who got up beside him. "Many thanks for your effort," he said in a dejected manner.

Zair Saihoud pressed the extended hand warmly, and with his free left hand he gave his friend an encouraging pat on the shoulder. "God is merciful!" he said in his gentle way.

Outside, it was dark and the air was swarming with mosquitoes. Abū Hasna, with bent head and slouched shoulders, walked back towards his house. With each step forward, the superstitious, calamitous thought of possible tragedy, of how life gives with one hand and takes with the other, weighed heavily on him.

8

The event was becoming a benchmark in the collective memory of the people of the marshes and beyond. It transformed into a sort of reference point in a timeline separating what was before and what came after. As for the disappearance of Hameed, it remained a mysterious case, but there was a unanimous conviction that the vanishing of the young man was a fortuitous incident. Many attempts of enquiry and search had been carried out in the whole region of al-Qurnah and also in other nearby towns. However, there was no trace of him. There were neither evidential signs nor clues as to his whereabouts or what happened to him. And as a local proverb would describe it, his disappearance resembled the melting of a crystal of salt in a bucket of water. But the issue did not stir up the population the way it should have. Indeed, it would have affected the people of the village differently—and tremendously—had it occurred during the idle days, before the appearance of the wali. But the miraculous event had eclipsed everything else.

The girl's health showed a piecemeal progress. Occasional visitors from other villages kept trickling in for some time. The parents concealed their concerns about Hameed for fear of relapse. However, the girl gradually became aware of the absence of her fiancé, although she kept silent. In addition to her natural timidity, she was expected to observe social norms that made it taboo for girls to show their intimate feelings. However, as the days rolled on, the inevitable moment arrived when the girl spoke her thoughts to her mother. "Where is Hameed, Mother? Did he get a new job somewhere? Has he heard about what happened?" she asked.

The mother, who was busy with her household work, was taken by surprise. She slowly turned around and looked at her daughter. There was the glare of expectation and hope in her wide, black eyes. The mother lingered in silence for some time as she did not know how to reply, which incited a look of apprehension on the girl's face. The mother did not miss the alarming signs on the visage of Hasna and dashed forward to strongly embrace her slim and fragile body. "He is somewhere and will be here soon," she comforted.

But the girl was not satisfied. She insisted, "Where is he, Mother?"

In involuntary response, the mother hugged the girl even stronger. "Do not worry, Daughter! We are all awaiting his return." With this indefinite answer, Hasna realised that nobody, including her mother, was able to answer her question. And this bitter conclusion tossed her into troubled silence. By now many weeks had passed by. The glimmer of realistic hope in the girl's heart gradually dwindled and eventually was replaced by a surrender to fate.

For a long time, Hasna had developed a habit that now had become almost a ritual. Each sunset, she used to touch, with a world of feeling and many sighs, the sky-coloured bed sheet that was neatly folded on the mahmal and which she embroidered for her wedding before she fell sick. Then with a doleful soul she would leave the house and stand by the edge of the water. Her heart bore supplication as her moist eyes surveyed the world at sunset: the still water, the motionless reed tops, and the vast crimson sky littered by a homeward-bound winged bevy of birds that flew low against the dim sky. She would spot, here and there, the spiralling columns of black-blue smoke while her ears captured the attenuated poignant tone of a shepherd's flute. All these elements were subjects of her familiar and beloved world, yet she felt a devastating forlornness. The sorrowful girl would strain her dewy eyes as though to catch sight of a lost entity. And deep in her heart, at the core of her mind, there was an aborted happiness, confiscated dreams, and forsaken hope. She would crouch on the wet soil, hide her face in her hands, and then convulsively sob as if to mourn till the end of time.

Woman with a Bike

For the last three or four years, and during my summer stay in the village family house, I used to see her almost every morning while I strolled in the heart of the surrounding forest. She biked along a narrow sinuous track that sneaks through the lavish foliage of the overshadowing trees and extravagant bushes. Whenever I heard the faint rattle behind, I stepped aside to let her pass. Her brief greeting of "good morning" came mixed with the faint sound of the brushing of her body against the extended boughs. She was a plain-looking person, a sort of working toiler woman in her late forties or early fifties. She made no particular impression on me, but I couldn't stop myself from wondering why she regularly followed this long, rarely trodden path that was strewn with forest litter. But certain things came up that one day I had a closer encounter with her. The outcome was painful and saddening. I am going to tell you what happened:

During the course of an early July morning I was pacing along the tortuous path that permeates the dimly lighted forest. The spell of the tranquil, mesmeric pleasure that seeped from the depths of the vestal thicket entranced me, and soon I found myself leaving the footpath and penetrating the arboreal realm. The trunks were mostly dark and excessively tall with interlaced crowns. The sky could hardly be seen, and the timid glitter of the oblique sunrays was obstructed from its sifting through the canopy. A pristine scent, which emanated from the dark brown soil and the thick mat of decayed branches and dead leaves of many seasons, filled the still air. I felt an esoteric rapture incited by the exoteric splendour of nature. I was spellbound by this secluded world, in which I sensed something primordial yet enchanting with clamouring solitude and the luring call of hypnotic silence as if the macro world of the forest was still in the lull of somnolence. After spending some time in this ritual-like wandering, I turned aside to join the winding path. Once there, I leisurely pursued my course, but hardly had I turned a crook in the track than my eyes caught the sight of a female figure some distance ahead. I immediately recognised her; she was the woman who came biking during my morning strolls. However, this time she was walking at a fast pace while dragging her bike next to her. I felt a drive to become acquainted with her, so I accelerated my steps and soon came up a short distance behind her. Upon feeling my footsteps, she startled, and without slowing her walk she partially turned her head with a shudder and widened eyes—a situation that almost made her tumble. I slackened my pace and hurried to comfort her with a smile. "Good morning, madam," I said.

"Oh! Good morning," she replied with signs of relief as she recognised me. Her round body was taught as though she was still on alert. I advanced a few steps and stopped, facing her. Thus far, I had caught no detailed sight of the woman, but now, in such proximity, I had a closer look. She had blunt facial features crowned by short light brown hair that barely touched the tips of her ears. Her pale, dry visage expressed an unmistakable stern look that was further revealed by her gaping little grey-green eyes.

"I am Denis." I introduced myself with intended informality while I watched her tightly closed lips and her vigilant stare, which disclosed what I thought her wariness.

She finally resolved to say in a toneless voice, "You may call me Irene." I shook hands with her, then I looked down at the bike and I observed the flat tyre; I noticed too that she had no repair kit.

"May I give a hand?" I cautiously presented my help in holding the bike, thinking that this would also render my company excusable.

"Thank you," she briefly said with an almost imperceptible quavering in her voice as if what I had offered was unfamiliar. I immediately stepped forward and gripped the bike's handlebar. I remained in my place, waiting for her to lead the way as the path was too narrow to accommodate us side by side.

By then, the life of the forest life pulsating. At intervals I could hear the chirping of finches and the poignant cooing of a distant pigeon. At one time I also heard the rustling of leaves that revealed a running squirrel. But we walked in silence that continued for some time, which made me somewhat uncomfortable, and I thought to myself that it was better to take the initiative and begin a common sense talk. "I used to see you biking this direction. Do you work in the plant nursery on the other side of the lake?" I said with a guess.

"Yes, I work there." She exhaled without turning her head and continued straight ahead. After this answer, silence prevailed for some time, during which I cast my eyes on the moving figure. She was admirably swift and agile, but her dynamicity intermingled with excessive alertness that seemed to contrast with the surrounding comatose world.

I dodged a dangling branch and meditated to myself on how to continue the conversation; the woman seemed reserved. "Have you worked there for a long time?" I finally managed to say and immediately felt the emptiness of my words, talk for the sake of talking.

But to my surprise she responded with a meditative tone, "Yes, I have worked in the plant nursery for a long, long time." She sighed and continued her course.

Ultimately, the density of the trees thinned and the path widened as the course funnelled towards the open space where the lake stretched. This allowed us to walk side by side, and it became possible for me to better observe her. Indeed, the more I looked at her, the more I felt her a lonely and introverted person. This didn't alienate me; on the contrary, it triggered fellow feelings and called me to socialise the atmosphere. However, her charmless aura sensitised me to adopt another line of conversation. "I come here every summer to the village family house," I said, glancing at her sideways. She remained gazing forward, separate from me and immovable as if I had not spoken a word, yet I continued, "I love this forested landscape and the lavish greenery, the morning scent of the woodland,

and the still lake." I said extravagantly to close, "What a wonderful world!"

This time she shook her head a little, and after a while she languidly pronounced, "Good for you!" in a tone lacking appreciation or affinity.

This conveyed a noncomforting message to my mind. *Was it nonchalance? A turned-off susceptibility to capturing the glamour of nature because of familiarity?* I thought to myself. This could have caused me to quit my endeavour to socialise with her, but I had irrepressible enquiry in my mind. For all the previous times and bygone summer seasons, and day after day of seeing her cycling past me, I kept asking myself why this woman followed this long, narrow, and markedly inconvenient path in the heart of the forest when there was a shorter road that connected the village with the other side of the lake. I determined to satisfy my curiosity before she arrived at her destination, which was looming in the distance.

By now the sun was well above the eastern treeline, and the lake gleamed and shimmered as it embraced the falling sunrays. Gliding waterfowl dotted the expanse of the still water, and some distance to my right, at the bank, there was a solitary oddly bent Tilia tree with its crown partially bathed in the water. Not too far away from that, in the direction of our apparent destination, I could see the arched wooden bridge embracing the two sides of the lake at the location of maximum narrowing. I looked again at my companion. Her pale hands were loosely clenched, and with a stern face she was steadfastly floating forward, soundlessly, voicelessly, and aloof from the surrounding world. All this weighed on me, and I dare say that I was not as cheerful as I was in the beginning, for her nebulous sombre mood had overshadowed my morning glittering sensations.

Needless to say, with each step forward my inquisitiveness became more pressing, but this was also paralleled by the challenging task of how to stir the idle atmosphere. We came within proximity to the plant nursery, and I thought it was time to enquire. "I wonder, why do you follow this rarely trodden and time-consuming forest path to reach your workplace?" I had put forward my long-lingering thought.

On hearing me, the woman, for the first time, slowed down her pace. Then she stopped and looked at me. I stopped, too, to face her bleary eyes, and I was startled by what I conceived behind them—an ashy world that made my heart sank. "Oh! That seems to you an odd choice?" she lightly protested with a pensive tone as she clasped her hands. I shifted my grip on the bike's handlebar and remained silent for a moment as I had no wish to respond immediately. There was a conspicuous change in her aspect, a sort of immersion reflected by her frozen look that passed beyond me and towards nowhere. This made me think that my question had stirred something delicate inside her.

"Evidently it is considerably more practical for you to follow the other, paved road," I explained, gesticulating towards the northerly direction. The woman appeared unsteady and indistinctly swayed as though touched by an invisible influx.

However, soon her shadowy state vanished, and she gazed steadily at me. The strong rays of the rising sun caressed her face, and her eyes fluttered. Then her lips eventually parted. "For the last twenty years

I have never followed that road," she pronounced in a hypnotised manner.

I cast upon her a questioning look, then I opened my mouth, but I stopped short of speaking as I thought it was wise to wait a little, to let her gather her thoughts. The woman turned around and resumed her walk, albeit slowly, and I copied her short footsteps with a mind full of anticipation as the intriguing nature of what she said was prominent. Then, following a period of silence, she spoke again: "That road witnessed the greatest tragedy of my life," she said sombrely in the manner of someone talking to themselves. "Twenty years ago, on my wedding night, I lost the love of my life in a car collision caused by a drunk driver. I nearly died too." She paused, crossed her arms, and turned her eyes towards me. Within them was a glazed look.

Yes, I remember well how her features lacked any discernible lively signs, as if the mould of her grief had been filled in with the wreckage of that distant bitter happening and had turned into rigidity cast with the occasional fracture here or a pore there from which her scathing sadness seeped. I listened silently. I didn't even have the desire to talk. After all, what meaningful words were there to address her with?

We reached the weather-beaten wooden pedestrian bridge. Side by side we slowly walked over the timber passage. There was a faint creaking sound that rose from the wooden planks. Halfway across the arched structure, my companion slowed her steps and then came to a stop. She turned her face towards me, but she wasn't looking at me. Then her lips parted. "From that time I have never followed a thoroughfare with motorised traffic." As she said this, she stepped diagonally to assume a semicrooked pose as she gripped the low barrier with both hands and looked towards the lake. "And since then I have never travelled in a car; I have never left my village except to go to my workplace," she resumed. Then she half turned and looked at me with dull eyes straight in the face. As if she were wailing, she sighed "Do you know now why I follow this forsaken footpath?"

I stood motionless, mesmerised and astounded by these successive pitiful, shocking revelations that left me unable to utter a single word. *What a life!* I reflected to myself. Before long, she straightened herself and extended one hand to grab the bike. Her eyes, as always, lacked glare or incandescence, and her vitreous aspect effectively concealed her emotional lacerations. "I leave you now. Thanks for your company and your help with the bike," she said with a faint smile as she held out her other hand. I nodded my head and silently shook hands with her. Then, with a rapid pace, she moved away. I kept watching her as she crossed the bridge and moved beyond, a forlorn and wistful being, till she disappeared behind the line of beech and oak trees that shielded the plant nursery.

The air was still fresh, and the blue sky was discretely ribboned with gossamer-like white streaks. I put my elbows on the guardrails and looked across the lake. On the far horizon there was white smoke curling up from a distant cottage chimney. And on the water surface the gliding birds were flocking, driven by habit and experience, under the bridge at the point where I was leaning. I looked at the waiting birds and murmured, "I have nothing to offer ... nothing at all."

Sorrow on the Banks of the Southerly River

Let me die among the date palms of the south
Let Mesopotamia be my last bed

It was the war era.[1] The epoch was truly a sad and turbulent time. I, despondent, sat in my tiny, brightly lighted room. The monotonous sound of the rotating fan breached the intense silence of that warm August evening. A few minutes ago I had heard disturbing news from the national radio. It was a military call-up of reservists, repeated three times in a high-pitched voice, which sent shivers down my spine. It meant I was summoned to join the army on the eastern war front. On hearing of the call-up, my body first recoiled and wriggled, and then I became transfixed in my seat as my mind started to analyse the dreary implications of what I had heard. It isn't an overstatement to say that what came to my ears embraced me in a suffocating grasp. I felt myself in a tragic state as if my life had fallen into ruin.

---

[1] Iran–Iraq War, 1980–8.

It was the third year of the war, a war that had become a prolonged period of bloodshed without any foreseen end. During these three years of continuous carnage, whole military regiments had been restructured as a result of heavy losses of life and tens of thousands of war prisoners. The army was principally based on conscription. Volunteers constituted but a small fraction of the combat forces. As the war went on, a recruitment crisis developed. To bridge the deficiency in human resources, the regime blocked demobilisation and announced successive reserve call-ups. Therefore, the military announcement that I had just heard was not unexpected. Yet even when someone expects an undesired thing, one still has hope for the opposite to occur, but now that slim margin of wishful thinking had vanished, and I was left facing the bitter reality, which threw me into a depressive mood.

As I steadily dived deeper into distress, my fingertips riffled through the stack of papers on the desk. My eyes were wide open, but I stared at nothing. My crestfallen mood called to my mind, with forceful gravity and annoying resonance, the saddening realities of the times, which shrouded everything. Fear spread its wings all over the nation, and terror assumed various horrifying incarnations: public executions of deserting soldiers and frequent raids of the military police and secret police on public places but also on people's homes to drive males to unidentified military training camps, not even sparing youngsters below the minimum age for military enlistment. Ultimately there developed an alarming decrease in males of working age, which was clearly mirrored by the scarce social activity and labour in the streets, in the markets, in offices, and in other public places. The frequent funeral processions of dead soldiers heading for Najaf,[2] and the ever-increasing number of mourning families, caused the situation to resemble a plague befalling a city. The burgeoning of condolence gatherings and funeral rites established a bleak atmosphere and implanted grief and sadness into every heart.

From within this distressful social environment there appeared limited yet tragic social behaviour. The regime, with enormous financial resources, offered large sums of money, land, and cars as compensation to people who had lost a first-degree relative on the war front, a policy that nurtured in some people a deterioration of ethics and looser morals as grieving the loss of a loved one had dwindled to a perfunctory minimum. All these depressing situational conditions formed the background of my distraught state. It was then that the sharp sound of collision of a flying cockroach with the windowpane plucked me from my inner thoughts and brought me back to visual awareness. My eyes purposelessly surveyed the confining space. On the ceiling and on the bare walls, paint of old age had lost its colour and was mostly replaced by whitish salt efflorescence. Exfoliated plaster was abundant in patches. Detached paint flakes could be seen on the poor-quality pitted mosaic pavement. Tiny cobwebs were nested in the corners of the low ceiling. The dull white silky traps were sprinkled with

---

[2] Najaf is the holy town and city of Shia Muslim clergy. It is also the location of a very large cemetery called the Valley of Peace, probably the largest cemetery in the world. This is why some call Najaf the city of the dead.

the dark exoskeletons of dead insects. On one of the walls there were two waiting geckos ready to prey on an unfortunate cockroach that was running across the wall. These were everyday, commonplace features of my room, but at that very moment they brought me an abhorrent feeling. The room looked like a repulsive and unpleasant place.

With an unsteady hand, I raised a half-filled glass of water that was on the table and swallowed it in one gulp. My immobile physique contrasted with my mind, which was in constant turmoil with a continuous ebb of flow of emotions and thoughts that couldn't be harnessed. *This is not my war* was the insurgent thought that insistently beat in my head and mirrored the escalating mutiny that surged up in my heart and mind. What made me feel so rebellious? I was inclined to think that my antipathy was not mainly the result of a natural psychological aversion to war and death but was principally related to my conscious refusal to die without a cause, a cause that I believed in. I realised that this situation seriously tested my principles. I saw myself as a conscientious objector to war. "I won't be dragged into this dehumanising struggle," I pronounced between clenched teeth. But that gust of ardour was soon wrapped by melancholy, nurtured by the fact that the challenge ahead would be tremendous and imminent. This troubling reality made me sink into sombreness. The view before my eyes went out of focus, and I found myself looking into a vacant, obscure space without shapes and without outlines, a mere accumulation of blurry eddies and interfering misty haloes, while my head was buzzing with an orphan question: *What is to be done?*

That was the crux of the daunting problem that engulfed me and for which an answer was desperately sought. But the more I turned that question around in my mind, the more I felt the menace of this dire situation, and along with that my anxiety swelled and adversely impacted my thought process. The combination of inner perturbation and giddying tension brought me a profound restlessness. I felt a need to move my body, perhaps to dissipate the accumulating pressure. I stood, came around by the table, and slowly shuffled my feet back and forth across the room. I paced the room for some time, then I stood by the window. Through the thin glass pane, which showed a hairline conchoidal fracture, I looked into the courtyard that was partially illuminated by a single hooded bulb that inefficiently lit part of the gloom; hence there was darkness galore. As my eyes absently gazed at the partially lighted yard, I made another effort to think clearly and to come up with a logical approach to dealing with this intricate situation. But the more I stressed my mind, the more I found myself incapable of putting together the fragmented thoughts that mirrored the pieces of a difficult jigsaw puzzle. *What is going to happen now?* I panicked. I turned around to once more pace the room to and fro. *What am I going to do?* I dolefully recycled the perplexing theme that wandered through the infertile landscape of my mind. Fact is, things were so mixed up in my mind that I didn't know on what to focus or how to concentrate; simply I wasn't thinking at all.

I sat down on my chair but soon rose to my feet again and walked about the room several times like a floating cork swirling in a whirlpool, a movement that made me feel somewhat unbalanced. To steady myself,

I stooped, putting my hands on the table, and closed my eyes for a short moment. I realised that staying within the confines of the four walls would plunge me more into more distress. Hence, I decided to leave and take a walk to ease my mind and burn off my tension, which might allow me to think clearly think an escape from this predicament. With this purpose in mind, I straightened myself, switched off the fan, and with slackened footsteps reached the unpainted wooden door and opened it. I extended my hand, turned the lights off, and closed the door behind me. I walked across the open courtyard that smelled badly. The source of the foul odour was the nearby squat toilet, whose door always remained ajar. But after a few steps, the motionless air smelled a bit better as it was mixed with a faint lemon scent that wafted from an orphan citron tree almost hidden in the surrounding darkness. Citron is an exotic plant species in the region, and its planting reflects a decorative tendency.

I crossed the courtyard and entered the narrow dark passage that led to the entrance door. I groped my way through the encamping gloom, and I experienced a short delay with the keys as I fumbled for the keyhole, but finally I turned the key in the lock and pulled open the door, which produced a low grating sound from the rusty hinges. I locked the door behind me and edged to the right in the narrow, semilighted street. The world breathed unpleasantly as the air was saturated by what it had inhaled of the obnoxious vapours from the open sewage channel that stank up the atmosphere. I walked slowly and cautiously because of the poor asphalt pavement that was full of potholes and detached slabs, which were difficult to discern in the dim light from the distant street lamp. Yet, despite stepping gingerly, I stumbled over something and trod on what I thought was an empty plastic bottle, which produced popping sound. Nearby, there were stray purring cats busy exploring the open rusty garbage tank, a scavenging activity that littered the immediate ground with tin cans and other refuse and increased the horrible stench of the air. On hearing the sudden sound, the poor animals frantically screamed, jumped out of the rubbish container, and disappeared in the folds of night.

Before long, I arrived at the junction with the main street, and once there, I lingered for a moment before I decided to head for the best part of town: the river[3] street. I always enjoyed walking at night. The night changed the face of the town. Besides the prevailing soothing serenity and cooler air, it concealed the shabby features of the town and wrapped it in an illusionary gown. Quietude reigned, though occasionally broken by the intermittent hissing of cockroaches and by the distant sole cry of a baby, which queerly deepened the stillness. The city had slipped into slumber before the right time. And if the city were a living thing with a soul, then I would say that this untimely sleep was its way of escaping the fears of the day and surrendering to delusional peace. Though I mulled over the deceitful face of the surrounding tranquillity, I nevertheless contemplated on how humans, in the cradle of sleep, abandoned the clatter and clamour of everyday life and acquired the meekness and placidity of a newborn.

To reach the river, I only needed to follow this single

---

[3] The Euphrates River.

trajectory, Freedom Street. It was a curious street name if one were to take into account the realities of the time and how freedom was a far-fetched dream. Indeed, the few main streets of the town that bore identifiers also had pompous names such as Revolution, Martyrs, Combat, and Struggle—terminology that reflected the political spirit of the times.

In the course of my dull walk, I passed by poorly lighted areas and several side streets. I cut across a large roundabout with a statue at its centre of a poet leaning on a staff whose petrified eyes gazed into nowhere. After ten to fifteen minutes I came within view of the lighted riverfront and the darkness beyond. Once there, I stopped for a moment and looked up at the sky. The open field of vision exposed a vast and wide firmament and a pathless, boundless starry domain. The tiny cosmic lights splashed all over the sky were cleaved by luminous, downy white galactic clouds vaulting across the sky with breathtaking splendour. The summer night sky had always been my fascination; hence, the scene should have been charming and calming as ever. But with the great turmoil that had befallen me, I sensed, to my regret, that this astral beauty had lost some of its effect.

I arrived at the bank of the river at a location near the new bridge. The river street started from this point and continued south-eastward. The bank to the north-west of the bridge was a wild strip of virgin land that was now hidden in sheer darkness. The street drew a wide swath, but with recurrent sinuosity that reflected the meandering of the river. This winding character set it apart from all the other streets of the town, which were characteristically straight segments that produced in an aerial view of the town the form of rectangles and squares. All along the contour of the pedestrian pavement there were regularly spaced light poles that cast a tortuous aisle of light, which decoratively dissected the opaque blackness. The light of the street lamps faintly exposed the bounding one-storey houses with low brick fences and frontal gardens that were mostly bathed in Cimmerian shade. On the riverside, the street lights indecisively reflected upon the dark waters, and their attenuation left the rest of the river in utter darkness, which complemented the comprehensive gloominess of the other bank and buried the extensive date palm orchards. For a second I saw, in the distant wall of impenetrable obscurity, the scintillation of a miniscule light, but soon it got sucked up by the impassable tenebrousness. The successive bright spotlights, within the immediate locale of the light poles, showed frenetic life activity. Flying and crawling insects of various sizes were buzzing, colliding, and preying on each other, while others had been attracted by the source of light and flew up high, got burned by the steaming light bulb, and fell lifeless. The light here had the internecine horror of a dark inferno.

With both hands in my side pockets and with my head slightly bowed downward, I slowly strolled on the rigid pavement, feeling myself being tremendously pushed by uneasiness and desperately pulled by my pursuit of solace. My mind was unmercifully slammed by tormenting thoughts, yet surprisingly I kept an eye open so as not to tread on stray insects. *What is to be done? How can I get out of this terrible plight?* These questions, unanswerable for now, drummed inside my head. It was both mentally exhausting and emotionally painful that I had no plan to follow. Embryonic thoughts died as soon as they were born. And it was distressing to realise that the stronger my determination to evade the war grew, the more my brain became disordered and barren of fruitful thoughts.

In an instant of ephemeral liberation from my inward obsession, I became aware of the peculiar solitude that surrounded me. *What consummate dreariness!* I thought to myself. There was an atypical airlessness. The surrounding environment seemed unusually dormant and sterile. It goes without saying that the dismalness of the surrounding milieu emerged by way of comparison and correlation. The river street, by virtue of its scenery but also given the exceptional municipal care, had always been the most pleasant and vivid place in the city, but now it was a rueful and forsaken location. Not only that, but also there was something menacing hanging in the air.

Naturally, my psychological state nurtured additional disturbing sensations. I had the feeling that I was walking through a deceptive quietude and a suspicious calm, that the encompassing tranquillity had a hint of latent activity and muffled clatter that could be unleashed at any moment. No wonder then that the somnolent atmosphere, which could have had a comforting effect, stimulated instead uneasiness and promoted a sense of lurking danger and fear of the invisible. *Am I delirious? Do I have morbid imaginations?* I questioned the soundness of my fears. Whatever there was in my mind, I knew that I was strolling at the wrong time and amid unsuitable circumstances. It also became clear to me that I wasn't going to experience the relief of mind relief and mental concentration that I had been seeking for. With that conclusion I might have retraced my steps and gone back home, but for some reason I held my course on the hard sidewalk, and soon I slipped once more into my inner turmoil.

On the ground of practical necessities, the principal problem sprouted into a plethora of challenging issues which all kept rattling around in my mind. If I opted to disobey the military call-up, then that would be a life-changing decision. Certainly I would find myself in a dire situation with quite grave consequences. The ruthless regime didn't often observe legal or juridical procedures to tackle the issue of both evasion and desertion of military service. Capital punishment had been uncritically applied in almost all cases that I knew of or had heard about. Some public executions had been carried out, and in some cases the families of the victims were forced to attend the execution. This had effectively terrorised people and was aimed to deter would-be slackers and deserters. In light of these fearful facts, it was clear that if I decided to refuse to comply with the military call-up, in a war I deemed immoral, then I would have to face the consequences. To escape the grim cost in case I might be arrested, I had to flee, and as there was no clear destination in mind for where to go in order to get away, I would have to hide for a period of time, during which I would be able to mull over the ways I might escape.

With only one week before the deadline to join the armed forces, my prospects were extremely pressing. "Hide where?" I apprehensively muttered to myself while feeling an intense wetness on my face and my hands, realising the immensity of the challenge.

Because of the unrestrained tyranny, panic had gripped the nation; hence I knew that nobody would offer refuge for a slacker or fugitive without risking their own life. This disheartening reality was accompanied by related annoying facts that jumped right off the top of my head. There was a travel ban with citizens being prohibited from travelling abroad at that time. Moreover, four out of the five surrounding countries had formed an undeclared war alliance, siding with the regime; hence they would not be safe havens even if I could manage to flee the country. This left me but with one escape route: through the war front. Moreover, I slowly felt that escaping my homeland would be a certain psychological burden upon me. The mere visualisation of myself becoming a refugee in a foreign country appalled me. It simply meant a drastic and unplanned change in the whole course of my life, and this "unplanned" aspect was quite a disturbance, for I was by nature of organised mind.

However, after a few moments, I found myself considering that necessity was the justification, and I convinced myself that I would keep my humaneness. I would keep in harmony with what I liked to live with. With this vindication I was able to persuade myself that the moral benefits of this serious decision outweighed the risks. This signalled a short mental heyday that temporarily distanced me from other distressing thoughts. But what really mattered now was to work out the details of the escape plan, knowing that bridging the chasm between intention and implementation was dishearteningly difficult. A fleeing scheme, given the circumstances of the time, was certainly a knotty task and a formidable endeavour. At every step, I could discern general, broad elements, such as the need for money, information, and contact persons, and securing these elements, besides other things, would require time that would not be available to me unless I hid for a sufficient period. This brought me again to the central point of where to hide.

As I reached this point of my anxious thoughts, which at that very moment represented an impasse, I found myself tossed into a pensive mood about the twists and turns of fate. Life appeared to me as a winding course with successive bifurcations; we decide at each bifurcation, small or large, to go on this trail or that. And I did believe that where I was standing was a major, decisive bifurcation that demanded great will and massive effort. I was at this vortex of solicitous thinking, which carried me, drifting far and wide on the shoreless sea of thoughts, when I found myself arriving at the first concrete staircase that led from the embankment down to the river. There were a number of staircases along the bank, constructed at points to serve as boat stops. But at that time of the year, the river water had considerably receded, exposing part of the river bottom that formed a marginal strip of land. So, at the location of the staircase I came to a halt. Sweat ran down my face and body. The muggy air brought with it a disagreeable sensation as my white shirt stuck to my skin. It was a peculiarly warm summer evening. I say peculiar because this desert fringe city usually experienced cool nights. This uncomfortable weather had reigned for the last three days, unabated. It was because of this inconvenient heavy atmosphere that I wished to reach the river and get a refreshing splash of water.

I carefully descended the small, low-rise stairs to finally set my feet on the dry riverbed. The nocturnal stillness was broken by the croaking of frogs living in relict ponds, which had been left behind by the retreated river. The exposed land strip, faintly illuminated by the nearest light pole, was dissected into polygonal mud cracks, which I felt rather than saw by the crispy sound of crushed mud curls under my feet. As I walked on the soft ground, I felt the presence of many tiny things, of flesh spewed by the river, and of glass and metal hurled by promenaders of bygone happier days. I advanced watchfully and walked slowly. With each step forward, the riverbed became moister and more rubbery with the emission of an increasingly intense foul smell. On my left side I could recognise the dark silhouettes of long reed plants, which became luxuriant near the edge of water. I advanced and soon reached the land–water boundary. The light from the street pole was considerably far away, but it still permitted the recognition of large things. There was the intense repellent odour of rotten things that hung about the place, deepened my downcast mood, and made me feel nauseous. For a moment I stood motionless and looked at the dark, silent river and the murkiness beyond. The quiet was deep and overarching, but it did not pacify my restive heart as I was unable to end the flow of ominous feelings. It was then, when I was about to bare my arms and squat to splash my face with the water, I heaved a shuddering sigh as I heard a languid sound—some sort of obscure movement.

I winced and a sinking feeling closed upon me, but I remained on alert. At first I wasn't sure from which direction the feeble sound had come, but on straining my ears and listening intently, I reckoned that its source was to my left, the direction of the tenebrous, reed-choked location. Lost in anxiety, I turned my eyes and stared, but there was nothing I could recognise at first sight. Then I decided to inspect more as curiosity overwhelmed me. I took a few steps in that direction and stopped to look and listen. In the tenuous light, and a few feet away, I dimly saw an anchored boat that was almost hidden by the vegetation. *Was it the sound of the boat's oscillation?* I reasoned first. Then I took another couple of steps. The moribund light feebly sifted through the dark reeds and barely permitted recognition of things, so I needed time to accustom my eyes to the darkness. Shortly after, my pupils had sufficiently dilated to permit me to inspect the view more closely.

There was faint rippling that caused a gentle rocking of the anchored boat. Inside the boat I barely discerned a veiled human figure, stretched along the bottom of the boat and wrapped in what I suspected to be a fishing net—imagine, in that heat! The view startled me, but I kept my ground. The head of the individual, as far as I could tell in the obscurity, was at the stem end of the boat and assumed a higher level than the rest of the body; apparently he was leaning his head on some sort of cushion. *So it was human movement,* I concluded. Then I took the last steps that separated me from the boat, after which I found myself at the bow. But at that moment my feet trod on a dry reed stem, and the ensuing noise alerted the person in the boat. He wriggled first then assumed a pose with the upper half of his body partly raised in the posture of someone poised to leap. I saw he had grabbed an oar in his right hand with his eyes fixed upon me. This startled me, and I remained pinned to my place. I stared at the vague body and sensed the person was strained and aghast. My gut feeling led me to believe that he was someone in hiding, a fugitive. This inference undoubtedly was nurtured by the overall conditions of the time and came to me with an enduring conviction like that of blind faith. This filled my heart with pity and clemency. I felt unity with this desolate, camouflaged person as I saw in him the miseries of so many people—and even the image of what might become of me in the near future! I stood still, not sure of what to do. The situation was embarrassing. I thought to myself, *Let me leave.* However, instead, I found my voice breaking the uncomfortable silence. "Hello!" I said gently with uncertainty stirring inside me. I waited for a few moments, but there was only silence.

Then, "Who are you? What do you want?" came in a low voice with a recognisably panic-stricken tone. The feeble light did not allow me to ascertain his outward appearance, so his voice communicated his state.

I was affected by the amount of anxiety and fear packed into his voice, and that made me hurry to reassure him: "Don't worry! I am taking a night walk." I wished to see the calming effect of my words on his visage, but I had no access to the minutiae of his facial features. Yet I could perceive that he was still on alert as I recognised that his body was set for some sort of action.

"Please don't stay here; it is better that you go!" he pleaded in an anguished, heartbreaking, and choked voice. He spoke at the time when many words were about to drop from my mouth. I stood still and remained undecided for a time.

Then I wisely thought, *I need not speak any more words or stay any longer.* I understood why he wanted me to leave, and I understood why he was so distressed. I sensed too, and once more, that there was something ominous in the atmosphere, something mournful and cruel. Indeed, I was capable of feeling and gauging the hovering danger in its full proportion. Without further ado, I turned around and hastened to leave the spot. I walked at a smart pace across the cracked riverbed and climbed the few steps that led me to the sidewalk.

Once there, I strode without vigour. The chance encounter that had just happened and the vision of the horrified man in the boat intruded upon my mind and triggered melancholic feelings. I had not refreshed my face with the river water, and now my face was streaming with sweat. I dried it on my sleeve. This combination of physical discomfort and mental solicitude overburdened my soul and body and increased my susceptibility to the void, queer surrounding environment. And with this, the sensation of insecurity and apprehensiveness came back with full potency. But I continued my stroll all the same, not because I hoped for betterment but because of sheer inertia. *Let me continue until the old mill of Beit E'jam, and from there I'll go back home,* I spiritlessly thought while gazing at the string of lurid light bulbs that aligned with the contour of the river, which were the only vivid sense of light in the sepulchral city.

Then, suddenly, something happened. I had no sooner crossed the interval between two street lights than I heard the distant sound of an approaching car, from behind. The vehicle smoothly lumbered down the street, which should have been gentle to the senses, but the emptiness and tension of the moment rendered that subdued movement into something startling, like the creepy motion of a slithering snake. I didn't turn my head to look. Maybe I dreaded the verification of what I unpleasantly anticipated, but such verification happened anyway. The car ultimately drove past me and stopped ahead at the next light pole. It was a black Mercedes with two rear antennas and a curtained back window These features were unmistakable identifiers: the car belonged to the secret police. With this recognition, my blood ran cold, for the secret police were an ill-famed bunch of vile, ruthless, and merciless people.

The car remained idling, and nobody immediately got out. I dragged my feet until I came in alignment with the motionless vehicle; then I involuntarily came to a standstill. My body was stiff, and my heart was wildly drumming in my chest. I had no sooner stopped than two men alighted from the car, one from each side, but for some reason they remained leaning on the open doors, staring at me. In my immobile, paralytic condition, I passively waited like prey waiting for the predator leap. As menacing signs were in the offing, I tried to summon all my courage. The open doors of the vehicle kept the interior car light switched on, which allowed me to get a glimpse through the rear side window. And what I saw made me shrink and tremble.

There was a man crumpled on the rear seat; he was lying with his face up. The sight spooked me. I was only able to see a raised knee and a head, the latter of which obliquely rested on the door. The proximity of the car allowed me to see clearly his facial expression, which bore the unmistakable imprint of pain and fear. Much to my panic, I also heard agonising, grievous moaning. He must have been mistreated and beaten before being thrown into the car. I stood shocked and horrified with my heart throbbing erratically. I didn't know how or upon what basis, but suddenly, amid my horrid feelings, a vague association sprang up, hinting that the miserable man reminded me of someone I had encountered. I had no time reflect on this hunch, because at that moment the two men slammed the doors shut, which blocked the distressing scene and the woeful voice from my senses, and both came towards me at stomping pace. Disheartened, astounded, and sweating, I had a foretaste of persecution and felt that something repugnant was imminent.

The light from the adjacent pole brightly lit up the scene. One of the secret police men positioned himself in front of me. He was short in stature and stout in build with a swarthy complexion, kinky hair, and a massive moustache, above which a large and ugly black mole rested on his right cheek. He had small, slanting eyes, which looked singular amid his broad, flabby face. His neatly combed, oiled hair made him atypical of men of his type. The phlegmatic look in his beady eyes was framed by a closed countenance that resembled the impenetrable gloom on the other bank of the river. There was something devastatingly bestial and awful in his opaque aspect that evoked a chilling feeling. The other one was taller and thinner with unkempt curly hair, a narrow forehead, and a peculiar pug nose— an appearance that would in different circumstances have brought a smile to my face. With reckless body movements, he assumed a slouched posture by my side, then immediately he shifted his feet one step farther away, which positioned him out of my direct sight. He almost glued his chest to my shoulder, and in that proximity his foul garlic breath blew down the side of my face. The two characters faithfully reflected the obscurantism that befell the time.

With a cold, aggressive glance, the sturdy one parted his lips. "Your papers," he dryly ordered with an intense charge of unscrupulous authority. At the time, whether at fixed or at flying checkpoints, one's personal identity card was not sufficient and needed to be accompanied by one's military service document.

I reached into my back pocket, pulled out the two documents, and handed them over with unpleasant anticipation. "Please …" I said in mellow tone but not without a tremor. Then I held my breath. Indeed, I thought that emphasising suave manners and civility as a defensive manoeuvre might restrain their expected aggressiveness, but that proved to be wrong reckoning. For a moment, the man's wolfish eyes remained fastened upon mine. Then he commenced, at first leafing randomly through the tiny military service booklet before starting his closer inspection, page by page, while intermittently staring at me throughout that short period, during which time seeped slowly. I felt numb with the worst expectations. The security policeman remained silent for a few moments, then he began gibbering to himself. I watched him turning the pages over and over again, mumbling the whole time, which made me think that he was doing this with a malevolent purpose, out of malice, part of his way of intimidating me.

Amid the cloud of uneasiness that enwrapped me, I noticed, not without dissatisfaction, that my hands made slight, almost unnoticeable random movements. I also realised that my limbs were trembling and that my knees had almost bent under me. To veil my condition, I tightly clasped my palms and squeezed my legs together. Peculiarly, the disquietude that stormed me didn't prevent my subliminal mind from dwelling elsewhere. It seemed that while my consciousness, during this short lapse of time, was strained by what would follow from the secret policeman, my subconscious was working on some other point: the grisly picture of the man thrown onto the back seat of the black Mercedes, a subject that clandestinely gnawed at my mind. This is why my brain suddenly relayed a message indicating that the man was the person who'd been hiding in the boat! The indication gushed strong and distinct, though it lacked clear-cut evidence as the encounter had taken place in poor lighting conditions. Yes, the hint was robust and convincing. *It is him,* I confirmed to myself, which left me flabbergasted. And along with this sudden identification, there sprang a whipping, torturing feeling of guilt. *It must have been because of me that he was arrested! They were watching me! They saw me talking to him … I am the one to blame.* And it crossed my mind that they might ask me about him point-blank. All these noncalming thoughts took but mere seconds, yet it was enough to leave me morally devastated.

Finally, the moustached man finished checking my papers. He extended his other hand in a twisted manner with no apparent purpose and unmercifully gazed at my face. His predatory looks had a shade of disappointment as though he had missed a game. "Your turn has come!" he said derisively and winked at his mate, who moved a little as if to make his snarling face visible to my eyes.

My turn has come?! What does that mean? I thought to myself, horrified. My lips quivered, but no words came from my mouth. The purport of his statement was ambiguous, but subconsciously I made an association and conjured up the distressing view of the tossed, beaten man in the car, and with that I felt a sinking within my heart. Undoubtedly a change had come over my aspect that did not escape the scrutiny of the men's unreadable eyes, but I exerted a massive effort to gather myself. "My turn has come?'" I enquired in a lifeless voice, feeling my anxiety rising to an even higher level while my bemused eyes caught a sarcastic wolverine grin on the thick, dark lips of the secret policeman, which was the first clear expression on his sculptured countenance.

"The military call-up of reservists," his voice came with a malignant tone. Paradoxically, on hearing his words I felt relief. I didn't know whether he perceived the easement that swept over me, but it would have been good if he had noticed that. Yes, my relative allayment was puzzling since his words, aside from being provocative in delivery, conveyed the very sickening and disturbing issue I was suffering from. But it was the nullification of the other, alternative meaning embedded in his obscure statement that temporarily pacified me. *They are not going to throw me in the back seat!* I thought to myself. But I knew that my trouble had only shifted from one level to another on the nightmare scale. I looked at the knitted eyebrows facing me, then I hurried to say, "Ah! The military service." I said, blinking, "Yes I'll join the ranks of the army."

As soon as I finished speaking, I felt a finger jabbing my shoulder, and I got a whiff of some offensive odour from the second secret policeman. "You are not scared about where they are going to send you?" the voice came in a provocative tone, charged with derogatoriness.

In reflex, my head turned a little sideways for a fraction of a second, but I could not get a full glimpse of the speaker. *The villain nettles me!* I uncomfortably thought while trying to keep myself immune to the small, cold eyes that kept scrutinising my face. I made up my mind to resist their vexatious demeanour; nevertheless, their harassment pressed on me, and I struggled, might and main, to control my growing anger. *I should restrain my emotions; one improper reaction and I will be lost,* I cautiously reasoned to myself.

"Scared about going to the war front, you mean?" I slowly said in a toneless voice just to gain myself time to come up with a proper response. "No, I am not scared; it is time to show one's national allegiance," I said with an emphasis that surprised me. My mind also worked the persuasion that what I'd said was warranted and was in accordance with the instinct of self-preservation, but it was not without self-resentment. What I pronounced was incongruent and in disharmony with my position. I reasoned to myself, *I could have said something else, a circuitous answer that would also keep me safe without infringing on my principles.* All this self-criticism lasted but an infinitesimal time.

"Oh yes!" The snub-nosed one laughed sarcastically, dragging me out of my inner thoughts. "Damn it! Here we have a hero!" he said, stomping the ground with his foot.

Meanwhile the moustachioed man seemed unmoved by what I'd said and kept a sulky face. "Droll, isn't it?" quacked the bully by my side. "He doesn't worry … what a man!" The scratchy, demeaning voice was deeply hurtful and blatantly indigestible. The cultural gap that separated me from these two men was so wide and profound that I found myself in a muddled and awkward position. I had no choice, no alternative, but to remain in a choking silence.

The dark, hideous visage that faced me finally broke its rigid mask and showed a wide, rascally grin. "Come on! Don't fudge! You worry, and you are afraid of going to the front, right?" His voice came in malignant tone while his greased hair gleamed as though reflecting all the rays of the street light.

They are ganging up on me, I distressfully thought to myself, detecting the large scale of their malicious tendencies and sadistic abuse, *What do these calloused men have in their personalities other than rudeness and predation?* I sadly reflected, conjuring up the role of these secret policemen in entrenching the oppression and tyranny that had turned people's lives into a nightmare. It was very trying to remain patient and curb my anger as I perceived how their scandalous shallowness made the underpinning of their arrogance unbearably galling and offensive. And at that daunting moment a silent outcry gushed from my soul: *Why does .evil dominate human life with merciless efficiency? Why does senseless cruelty have such power and authority?* Yet I had to endure.

The tall secret policeman deliberately swayed his body to and fro, and with each forward movement his chest collided with my shoulder, sending me into feeble, almost indistinct oscillatory movement, which increased my vexation. But I had neither the nerve to shift my position nor the spirit to look at him over my shoulder. Then, with suddenness, the pendulum-like movement stopped, and I felt a heavy clapping on the shoulder, which caused me to shudder. "He is afraid! I swear thrice[4] he is afraid!" the pug-nosed one asserted mockingly, performing his concordant role in the persecution game, which both men pursued with a peculiar relish.

I was at the end of my tether. The experiences of this doleful evening had brought me to the nadir of my tolerance, and I felt my morale drastically depleted. Spiritless and mentally strained as I was, my eyes, whether consciously or unconsciously I can't tell, shifted up and gazed at the garnished sky; it was very rich with jutted stars, but I felt the lanterns of perpetuity lacked their usual soothing inspiration. Moroseness, discontent, and sorrow had undoubtedly disrupted my capacity to feel what I usually took to be sublime and beautiful. More painful to me was that I felt my psyche altered in how I viewed things, for I perceived in the firmament not the usual inspirational poetic realm but the brute physical reality: a lethal cosmos and hostile space of cold and fire. With a sore

---

[4] Swearing three times is considered, traditionally, to be the strongest assertion.

heart and harrowing self-denouncement, I lowered my eyes to meet the dark wolfish face. He was looking at me with venom overflowing in his eyes, waiting for my verbal reaction, possibly to catch a desired, yet missing, clue. *They are trying to prompt me into committing a slip of the tongue.* I was still able to think rationally. Reflexively I compressed my lips as if in fear of the flow of my true feelings. I wasn't a gaffe-prone person, yet who knew what could happen under this unrelenting pressure from two sides—rather, from all sides. "No, no … I have no worries and no fear; it is the call of duty," I responded, realising again that I was complying with the exerted bullying and intimidation, for which I denounced myself, though with accompanying ameliorating thoughts. Was it unjustified self-judgement? But this retraction didn't lessen the growing feeling that I was on a downhill course.

When I finished my response, I imagined seeing the shadow of vulturine lustre floating on the face of the malicious surly policeman. He tilted his head to one side, parted his lips, and spat on the ground. "He seems to be good citizen," he derisively hissed with immovable countenance.

The other one gurgled noisily. "I guess you mean he is a patriot!" he said in a harmonised derogatory manner, laughing provocatively.

I stood motionless, but there was great turbulence inside me. "They have gone too far," I chokingly muttered to myself, knowing that I had no means to ward off their mischievous, irreverent behaviour. I needed a herculean effort to restrain myself. I felt spasms in my neck, sensed a peculiar odour in my nostrils, and felt a dryness in my throat, the sort of unique signs that one experiences when on the brink of desperate action, but I remained stiff as a statue. I hated their villainous demeanour, their gross meanness, their overt sordidness, and their egregious bullying, but I also abhorred my inability to express, at any level, my inner feelings. And I detested my conforming replies even more. It is an exceptional and extreme moment of life at which one suffers from a paroxysm of moral anguish that calls for immediate nursing and soothing that isn't available.

"Go home now! Do not stay around here," the dark-hued man dismissively ordered with a contemptuous grimace while handing back my papers. He wiggled his moustache and made a slight eyebrow gesture to the other one, who smote me with his hand on the back. Then both of them turned around and walked away with sardonic laughter cleaving the deadly silence, as though celebrating my diminishment. When they reached the car and opened the doors, I saw once again, for a split second, the appalled face and heard the clogged moaning—and with that a chill gripped my heart. "The poor man! What terrible infliction I brought him!" I groaned guiltily with a sorrowful perception of how the delicate interplay of fortuitous occurrences, random events, and situational elements bring unexpected twists of fate and reshape one's destiny. The black car slowly crawled away. It looked like a prehistoric giant insect, satisfied after swallowing its prey whole.

High up in the adorned sky there suddenly appeared an eye-catching, short-lived, bright trace of a falling meteor. Along the river, the light of the street lamps shimmered tremulously on the proximal waters. I stood unsteady and numb, utterly stranded in the middle of nowhere. I felt frail and wasted as grimness grabbed my split self and my divided soul. There was drumming in my head and a swinging of the scene before my eyes. I raised a hand to my forehead and closed my eyes, and for a few moments I stood still. Then, after a time, I regained my balance, but I had no thoughts and no mental struggle as if the cauldron of external events and internal turmoil had drained me of all my mental energy. At length, I opened my eyes and slowly moved my feet to cross the river street. Soon I got sucked in by the lifeless, semidark veins of the entombed town.

Reminiscences of Childhood

My Village, My World

Remembrance of childhood events usually comes faint, foggy, and subdued. It also comes with a strong nostalgic flavour that is embedded within a blurry, dilated framework of time. But the specific segment of my memories that I am speaking of here has a different aspect. These memories hold a strong wistful component, and for reasons I can't decipher, they have an unusual clarity as if they had been engraved on a piece of slate with an echo that has reverberated, nonattenuated, down the years. However, I am aware that my adult mind inevitably leaves hues and shades behind as I weave this tapestry of that bygone childhood world.

I call to mind my small village,[1] the low adobe houses, the dusty narrow streets with the central one dividing the village into two symmetrical parts. Other than the agglomeration of densely packed straw and clay weather-beaten houses, there were but few aspects worthy of mention. The school, limited to the primary

---

[1] Rustamiyah village, east of Baghdad City, now demolished.

stage, was located at the southern limit of the village. The classes, flimsy dim rooms, assumed an open rectangle plan that was surrounded by an earthy, unequipped playground, which was in turn bounded by closely spaced Hoor[2] trees. There were a few sporadic grocery shops in the village, and these were confined to the main street. The lone cafe in the village had a wide front yard partially covered by a fixed awning made from date palm fronds and supported by four wood trusses. During the late afternoons on the boiling summer days, the cafe boy kept sprinkling the yard with water from a metal jug to gently wet the warm, dusty ground and thus bring about a cooling of the air. What made a particular impression on my mind was the large, white, battery-operated radio, which I observed and heard whenever I walked past the cafe, as it was positioned, during the afternoons and evenings, on a small exterior wooden shelf. This was the first radio in the village, and it remained a focus of public attraction for long time. There was single hairdressing shop, called Abd barbershop after the name of its owner. It was the most elegant place in the village. The hairdressing shop was a long, low cabin built of adobe, yet its finishing, its inner atmosphere, and its delicious fragrance rendered it different, in a wonderful way, from all other places. Instead of logs and mats, the roof was made from corrugated metal. From inside, the bare straw mud walls were covered with white plaster. On the walls there were hung pictures of women wearing flashy make-up with unfamiliar dresses, pictures of scenery, and images of brightly coloured birds. The wooden

---

[2] Abele trees.

commode that held the shaving mirror had shelved perfume bottles of various sizes, shapes, and colours, which I remember particularly well. Whenever I went to have my hair cut, and because of my small physique, I was seated on a plank of wood set transversally on the armrests of the chair. As soon as the barber started his work, he pressed my head downward; hence my sight remained fixed on the lines of those fancy perfume bottles most of the time! But of particular interest was the manually operated ceiling "fan", which was a local invention due to necessity as there was no electricity available for domestic use. The "fan" was made from large rectangular cotton-stuffed cloth that lolled, by means of a rope, from a metal pulley attached to the ceiling and was moved, in a pendulum-like motion, by the other end of the rope, which was held by the next waiting customer, who sat on a chair beside the entrance door and did the repeated pulling and releasing of the rope. The to-and-fro movement of the stuffed cloth over the shaving seat provided a current of air for the barber and his customer.

These few facilities of the village hinted at an insipid life. But such a dull impression naturally did not cross my mind for it was my sole world, the only world I knew, and I found it full, picturesque, and extremely enjoyable, especially when I added those natural elements that surrounded the prosaic agglomeration and which constituted the part of the milieu of my playing and entertainment. At the northern limit of the village there was a narrow irrigation ditch with a number of widely spaced water regulators. Along this narrow ditch, I used to crouch and intently watch the newly hatched black tadpoles, thinking them tiny fish. And not far from that ditch there was, in parallel alignment, a row of tall, crooked date palm trees that held, during the warm months, heavy golden date clusters. More to the north, and a short distance from the line of date palm trees, there extended an obnoxious evergreen wall of oleander shrubs with their unkempt leafage and pink poisonous flowers forming an effective deterrent against trespass of the military academy terrain by the village's domesticated animals. On the north-eastern corner of the village, there was a giant eucalyptus tree that now occupies a special place in my memory—and this is not solely related to its iconic character, which made it distinct among its peers, with its swaying head towering over everything I knew in that world of the past. The eucalyptus was also my favourite surveillance place during the long summer season. During the school summer holiday I used to climb, barefooted, the trunk of the tree, which had tremendous girth. I raised my dishdasha[3] to the waistline and fastened the hem firmly so as to have more freedom of movement for my legs. Then I clenched my fingers around whatever knot or bump was afforded me by the callused trunk, moved my feet to find a firm place to stand on the rough, fissured body, avoiding the unstable exfoliated bark, and thus gained safe footing for good leverage and pushed myself laboriously upward. As I climbed, my eyes frequently came almost in contact with the two-way trails of persistent ants that exploited the clingy resin, which became partially crystallised with the yellowish-orange hue that marked the wounds of

---

[3] A long, light loose dress with long sleeves.

the great tree. My target in this ascent was somewhat modest. In fact I lacked the sufficient bravery and had no stamina to venture up higher than the intermediate branches. My destination was always confined to a large limb that extended first horizontally and then bent obliquely upward, making a natural design that afforded an excellent seating place.

Once I settled my body on the lofty grand branch, gasping for breath and partially shaded by the luxurious foliage, I Leant my back against the rising part of the crooked bough, extended my legs, and remained still for some time to regain my regular breathing and to slow my thudding heart. In the scorching, oppressive heat of summer, this covert refuge appeared to have an Elysian touch. From my position there, my senses relayed various messages. Above me and through the entangled branches I could see but tiny patches of the brilliant blue sky. Obliquely, I saw the western plain, dotted with bushes and shrubs, which yielded an extensive spotted pattern that seemed utterly empty and desolate with occasional whirlwinds chaotically dancing across the dappled landscape. When I turned my eyes elsewhere, I caught sight of other elements in the surroundings: I saw the high artificial trapezoid earth hill that served as the training shooting field for the students of the military academy. This was an attractive location for me and other children. We used to go there after the end of each shooting exercise to dig out and collect the buried lead bullets and then hurry home with our little warm trophies. We melted them and poured the liquid metal into whatever water-filled utensil, some sort of childish casting, to gain solidified forms of various and complex shapes that we likened into intermingled human figures and animal shapes. And sometimes we cast the melted lead in mud moulds to have specific forms that we used in our games.

The next view that my eyes would catch was the low mud fence that surrounded the stables of the army cavalry unit, which looked empty as the horses were led back to their stalls. This particular place is associated in my memory with festivity as it was the starting point for the fantastic annual event of jackal hunting. Every year, on one of the late spring days, a jackal hunting event, which was not a native activity, commenced in the late morning. The riders, both English and Iraqi horsemen, wore fascinating clothing of black caps, scarlet coats, white trousers, and long brown boots, all of which in my mind represented fabled attire that had no resemblance to anything in real life. I also recall how the large group of hunters, accompanied by restless saluki hounds and headed by a nomad cavalier called Nashmi, who had a curiously large moustache, started their march slowly, and we the children, thrilled and excited, followed, barefooted, close on their heels. Then the procession gained speed. The horsemen shook and swung their whips in the air with a cracking sound, and soon the gaits of their horses changed from walking to trotting and finally into galloping with the hammering hoofs ploughing the earth. The hounds howled incessantly as they ran, at full speed, ahead of the large hunting band. With this rapid change of pace we began, with joyful faces enveloped by the raising dust, to run to cope with the departing pageant, but the race was too swift, and soon we were left far behind. So, with the spurting frustration of aborted joy, we slowed down and finally stopped, panting and gasping, as we watched the horses and their riders disappear among the faraway trees, shrubs, and bushes.

With this colourful image in mind, I would turn my head away from the stables and shift my sight downward to where the village water tap was located, not far from the eucalyptus tree, which also marked the commencement point of the subsidiary lateral ditch, along which there was a line of willow trees casting interlaced cool patches of shade. Their dangling leafy branches and twigs resembled, to my childish mind, the loose long hair of bent-over mourning women,[4] but with a queer green colour. The other side of the ditch was lined with a matted fence of myrtle shrubs that delineated part of the eastern border of the village. With this exhaustive visual perception of the surroundings, my other senses emphasised their role and came to the forefront. In the sea of high noon silence my ears received, with rapt attention, the subdued whisper of nature embellished by a few sounds. The sad cooing of a pigeon, sitting somewhere on the highest branches of the tree, set my soul afloat on enchanting ripples. I could not resist the temptation to indulge in the pleasure of vocal interaction, so I cupped my hands around my mouth and imitated the pigeon call. Then I fancied hearing the reverberation of both the birdsong and my voice, intermingled in a heart-capturing, rhapsodic melody, before they dispersed and vanished in the folds of the diurnal silence. And from among the lush leaves

---

[4] In traditional mourning gatherings, and as a sign of grief, women repeatedly bow their heads and let their hair dangle while screaming and beating their breasts.

and lavish branches there came a faint flutter and the lovely twittering of nestlings that made me raise my head to catch the view of a sparrow hovering around a hidden nest. But soon the voices of this avian family faded and finally died out to allow my ears to capture the most subtle tone of nature: the whisper of a breeze that caused a feeble rattling of the tiny green-crimson leaves. I heard the soughing of sporadic gusts of light wind sifting through the profuse twigs that danced laxly in response. These delicate moans, sighs, and quivers of nature, impersonal as they were, wrapped my soul in poignant, rapturous, and mystic feelings that defied verbal explanation. In such an elated state, I reached for the delicate, succulent leaves and rubbed them between my fingers, feeling their sap wetting my fingertips while a sweet fragrance filled the air.

Abboud

It was noontime one July day, amid the midsummer period of scorching heat. The air was dead still. Both land and sky were dormant and without visible sign of life or activity. No human walked, no creature on four feet moved, and no bird flew. The only sound that I heard was the buzzing and scratching that came from the struggle of a tiny grasshopper that I had shut in an empty matchbox and put into my chest pocket, which was one of my pastimes. In this seemingly forsaken world I climbed the huge eucalyptus tree and occupied my usual place on the rough bent branch. From there, I watched, like a vigilant sentry with a peculiar obsession, the figure of a solitary man who ambled his way down the dusty route that led from the distant thickets along the banks of the Diyala River. I knew him by name; he was Abboud, a silent and lonely person who appeared once a day almost always at the specific time of midday when the world looked utterly vacant, abandoned, and forlorn. My watching, day after day, of the man in his constant appearance fabricated in my little mind a strange belief, a fancy that he led an eternal peripatetic existence. More perplexing and intriguing to me was that I always saw him moving in one direction. He appeared from the distant eastern arboured strip that adjoined the river, and he disappeared from my sight at some point beyond the western limit of the village, where the vast wasteland started. I never saw him passing in the reverse direction nor on any other course at any other time of the day, which made him look like a regular daily voyager on a repetitive one-way journey from nowhere to nowhere. This unusual impression nurtured wild, scary imaginations. I had a predilection for believing that the enigmatic aspects of Abboud's appearance expressed and defined his personal eccentricities, which embodied something creepy and repulsive. Along this line of uncomfortable reasoning, it appeared natural that I felt a growing incertitude about his identity and suspicion about his tasks in life, which gradually made me think, with an ample amount of apprehension, that he had sinister intentions, and that he was carrying out an obscure, mysterious errand that might have a connection to the fearsome Abd al-Shatt![5] And this extreme thought was not totally without any supportive element for I had heard from my mother, in her winter tales, that this gruesome creature stealthily paced the dense bushes that bordered Diyala River, the direction from which Abboud always appeared! As for real observations and factual details, I remember but few things to describe the man. He was a shabbily dressed person with a dishevelled appearance, a man clad in humble pale khaki dress—baggy trousers and a wide dangling shirt. He wore a pair of military boots and gaiters into which he tucked his trousers. His side pockets were conspicuously bulgy, and we, the children, often wondered about what he stuffed them with. He wrapped his head with a handkerchief to protect himself from the burning midday sun. He tightened it in a peculiar way with knotted corners that bore a resemblance, in my mind, to four little horns, a feature that undoubtedly added to my uneasiness. He kept his head slightly down in the manner of a person lost in thought. His left hand was invariably behind his back, while the right one remained free, dangling at his side. His stooped shoulders rendered him somewhat gibbous in profile, but he had a sturdy frame and a steady pace, and his strides were impressively robust. Filled with entangling feelings of aversion, apprehension, and curiosity, I kept watching him closely as he came slowly down the empty road, and

---

[5] Abd al-Shatt is a mythical character who dwells near rivers and has the capability of extending his height and becoming considerably taller. He captures his unfortunate victims and drowns them deep in the river.

when he arrived at what I considered an appropriate distance, I shared the information with my mates, who awaited my signal down on the ground, beneath the adjacent blackberry tree. I laid a finger on my lips: "He has arrived!" I hurried to say and hastily climbed down the tree.

We huddled behind the formidable trunk and watched Abboud with intense gravity. And though we were stormed by hardly repressible, puerile and malicious feelings, we neither made a movement nor released a sound lest he recognise our presence. He usually walked without turning an eye, and this brought us assurance and a feeling of relief; yet his nonchalance was unusual and even disturbing as though he were separated from the surrounding world—and this bestowed upon him an air of unpleasant mystery. Ultimately, this period of coerced latency came to an end when Abboud reached the first rusty water regulator of the irrigation ditch, at which point the squeak of his shoes completely faded away. At that particular instant, our suppressed obstreperousness broke loose and we became glaringly rowdy, shouting and throwing stones and dry twigs towards him. None of us showed gentleness towards him. Unaccountably, he showed but mild response in reaction to our unprovoked rudeness and nastiness. He paused, turned through half a circle, and looked towards us. He spoke no word and moved no limb, and when we observed him in that position we became startled, we frantically ran away.

Fact is, we did not know anything about him. On reflection from an adulthood standpoint, I believe that the flicker of hostility was motivated by an ambiguous sensation of alienation that grew out of his solitude, folklore tales, and childhood naughtiness, which dictated our behaviour. I recollect how once I casually heard my father chatting with some people and referred to Abboud as a widowed and reclusive person. At the time I did not know what the words *widowed* and *reclusive* meant, but I disliked them all the same, for it just occurred to me that it was unpleasant for a person to be assigned such ambiguous adjectives, which further added to my worrying thoughts about the man! Oh childhood fancies and vagaries!

The Sweets Seller

It was midmorning, yet the heat of the day had become uncomfortably high. I squatted on the dry soil, entertaining myself with hunting the *ghzayel*.[6] In this enjoyable game I used a piece of sewing thread to hunt the concealed tiny insect that buried itself at the bottom of an inverted conical burrow which had smooth, steeply graded sandy walls. I held the thread with my thumb and index finger and slowly lowered it into the beautifully engineered burrow, taking much care so the lower end of the thread wouldn't touch the sloping wall to avoid premature collapse of the sandy cone. When the thread touched and then slightly penetrated the fine sand at the inverted cone apex, it started to shake and tremble, indicating that the insect had caught the end of the thread as it mistakenly thought it to be trapped prey. When this occurred I carefully

---

[6] Ant lion.

pulled the thread upward—and hurrah! I watch the dusty catch struggling feverishly in a funny manner!

While I was absorbed by this hunting game and moving from one conical trap to another, I heard the high-pitched horn of a car. I raised my head and saw the arrival of the wooden bus, the sole transport vehicle that connected the village with Baghdad city. The bus made two round trips daily. The driver usually waited for two or three hours before leaving as this time was necessary to have sufficient passengers. Unlike the rough military vehicles that I commonly saw around, the bus had a different character and bore attractive features. There was a large bundle of swaying peacock feathers fixed at the tip of the engine bonnet. On the bus exterior there were coloured paintings and writing. I particularly remember a large drawing, on both front doors, of a flying eagle capturing a snake in its beak. The vehicle's interior was even more embellished. Above the windscreen there was ciliated ribbon with a silvery lustre, and slightly below it there hung a series of tiny, bright yellow brass bells. There were numerous pictures of women with florid complexions in exotic natural scenes stuck to the sides and back of the bus. Some of these even extended to partially cover the wooden top part as the bus had no headliner. There were also elegant colourful graphics and writings interspersed here and there. Dandling tiny dolls and blue and green lamps could be seen on the successive transversal trusses of the ceiling. These added a gleeful atmosphere and rendered the bus into a wonderful and charming object. For me, these extravagant decorative elements were an appropriate aspect that befitted a vehicle that was associated with the magic and charm of the capital city.

I was particularly enamoured by the vehicle during its evening return trip that I had acquaintance with whenever opportunity offered itself to accompany my father on his monthly shopping visit to Baghdad. During these sporadic nightly bus rides, a melodious wave and a dreamy, vague atmosphere overwhelmed me. As the bus rolled on, its headlights smoothly infiltrated the wall of darkness. It swayed and rocked at turns and at crossings of dry channels that dissected the monotonous plain, and with this sideways and up-and-down movement, the tiny brass bells jingled softly, deepening the slumber of the fatigued passengers. As I sat on the lap of my father, I resisted the power of sleep and remained wide awake. I leant my face against the windowpane and felt the coolness of the night. Then I gazed, through the thin glass partition, upward and felt that I was enchanted by the magical pulsating glitter of the stars. I lowered my eyes to the level of the concealed horizon to catch sight of the distant scattered clusters of terrestrial lights, of places and locations that seemed strange and unfamiliar as if they were unrelated to my everyday world, for the pitch-darkness bestowed remote incandescent objects with a legendary touch and a fabled aspect. It simply occurred to my mind that the world of the night was completely detached from the world of the day; the two appeared different realms, unrelated entities: the clear, discernible world of the day contrasted with the formless, mysterious, semimythical world of the night, where the mute dimness carried an eerie silence.

When I slightly opened the window, a whiff

of breeze, impregnated with the wild fragrance of prairie vegetation,[7] brought hypnotic effects. All these intangible components granted the aphotic world of the night an inscrutable, mesmeric charm, which enhanced my state of mind rich with hints, symbols, and forms akin to the imagery of what I recognise now as extrasensory perception.

With these visions and impressions, I watched the bus approaching at high speed, a cloud of dust trailing behind it, before it slowed down and finally parked obliquely in the meagre shade of the twin date palm trees not far from where I squatted. I watched the passengers leaving one by one to fetch their luggage, some of which was in bundles fastened by a rope on top of the metallic roof of the bus that reflected the falling rays of the sun with a strong luminance that blinded the eye. As the passengers were leaving the vehicle, the hefty driver raised the engine bonnet, then hurried with a bucket, which he filled with water from the nearby canal, to cool down the simmering radiator that hissed with a sizzling sound.

But I kept watching attentively the disembarking passengers until I saw a tawny-skinned lean man get off the bus. Then I stood up with a smile. He was the seller of the peculiar "stork egg"[8] sweets. It was Thursday, and he only came on this day of the week; therefore, I was expecting him and awaiting his

---

[7] These include *aqool* (*Alhagi graecorum*), *awsaj* (*Lycium shawii*), and *tartai* (*Schanginia aegyptiaca*), which are species of dry land vegetation indigenous to the Middle East region.
[8] A foamy, porous sweet made from boiled sugar and colour additives. It is almost nonexistent today.

appearance. Being from Baghdad with a load of these unfamiliar sweets was an aspect that granted the seller, whom we never knew by name, a privileged place in our tiny hearts. But that was not all. In stark contrast with Abboud's personality—and it was significant that I made this comparison—the Baghdadi seller was talkative and pleasant with a perpetually smiling face. From the moment he set his feet on the ground, an air of joyfulness surrounded him while his face had a cheerful cast. He got off the bus while holding a folded, long-legged stand in one hand and a wide metal tray, covered with a pale pink conical hood, in the other. As soon as he set his feet on the ground, the sweet seller hung the stand on one shoulder and put the tray on his head. Then he briskly walked away from the bus. I always wondered about, and admired, his skill in balancing the hooded tray without the support of his hand during this agile walk.

My friends and I cheerfully and ceremoniously approached him, and we accompanied him as he moved towards his usual selling point, the umbrageous location under the eucalyptus tree. As he walked, he sang, with extolment, of his sweets for sale in a melodious and artful way, while his graceful body movements went in rhythm. In chorus, we merrily joined in his patter until he reached the ample shade. Once there, he stopped, brought down the tray, and rested it on the tripod light stand. During this very brief procedure, our eager eyes watched the veiled sweets with impatience. The veil fabric was translucent, allowing us to distinguish the blurred irregular contours of the heaped sweets.

We had already prepared our small coins, one anna[9] or smaller coins, in our breast pockets, so when he straightened his body and looked at us with a wide smile, we hurried to hand him the money and got one piece or two of the "stork egg". But he was generous, and that was an additional virtue that made him dearer to our hearts. He used to keep us near him for a long time, during which he addressed us with questions that we willingly and competitively answered for the prize of getting an extra free piece of the tasty sweet.

It happened one day, while accompanying my father to a postfuneral gathering, that I overheard the elderly people labelling this joyful sweet seller as "a sly sleuth with the smile of a fox". The words *sly* and *sleuth* were not yet in my vocabulary, but they struck my mind with a sort of appreciation. The reference to his smile seemed even more praising because whenever he parted his lips, which he did almost constantly, I saw a glitter from two golden teeth, which was a unique feature as nobody else I knew had such impressive dental scintillation.

The Flood

The summer season came to an end, and the dust whirls were no longer there. The short, indistinct season of autumn passed almost unnoticed and was followed by the long, bleak, cold winter. But with the

---

[9] Anna was a currency that remained in circulation till 1958. Seemingly the name was adopted after the British Indian anna. In Iraq, one anna equalled four fils.

arrival of spring, events began heading for a tragic turn that eventually translated into a phenomenal event.

It was one day in April. The air was mild and fresh. There were patches of solitary white clouds that sailed imperceptibly in the blue sea of the sky. It was not yet midday when the school principal suddenly instructed us to go home and added that the school would be closed for an indefinite period of time. This was surprising because it was an untimely interruption of our school days and an unscheduled closure. But the surprise was immediately superseded by the joy of having an unexpected holiday. Consequently, we pupils left the school with euphoria.

But on my way home, my mirth was gradually diluted. As I leisurely walked down the central street, I observed uncommon and alerting scenes. Hither and thither people huddled in small groups, conversing. The narrow side streets were unusually congested with people. Doors of many houses were flung open to reveal their occupants bundling and packaging their luggage. The grocery shops, the cafe, and the barbershop were all closed. When I lingered near a group of agitated women, I heard one of them telling the others that she had heard the creepy call of a raven in the early morning, something I did not understand at the time but which later I took to mean a portent of misfortune and fatality.

As I continued my way homeward, I increasingly sensed that the atmosphere was freighted with hidden menace. When I finally arrived at home, I saw the same odd activity and perplexing irritation. My father, a staff member of the military academy, who should have been on duty at this time of the day, was at home. At variance with his calm manner, I saw him tense with a hurried pace. He held things and transferred them from the rooms to the yard while my mother, assisted by my elder sister and brother, was engaged in baling and packaging things. As I stood facing this confounding situation, the remaining portion of my original cheerfulness evaporated and was replaced by rueful amazement. I found myself enveloped by a cloud of unknowing that seemed to conceal something obscure and perilous, something akin to hostile opacity. Under the weight of this cryptic frenzy, my body started to shrink. I leant my back against the wooden pillar of the backyard shelter and stared, with startled eyes, at the ongoing fuss in complete stupefaction. My confusion and frightened look did not escape the attention of my elder brother, Hadi, who came hurriedly, grabbed me by the shoulders, and in a vibrating, excited voice uttered a few words that deciphered the enigma: "The Diyala River will flood the village! The flood! We must leave!"

The flood! I had no clear notion of the dimension of the threat that a flood might represent. But the Diyala River, yes, I knew for sure! It was the direction from which Abboud came! And that was enough to toll the bell of warning for me. In the late afternoon of that day, many families, including mine, took refuge in the large multistorey building of the military academy that had been left empty because its occupants, the academy students, had joined the army in a massive effort to prevent the incoming flood from drowning the capital city, Baghdad. Of course, the building could accommodate just a portion of the village population. I had no idea where the rest of the people had fled.

Those who had been afforded a place were instructed to spend the night in the unoccupied dormitories of the first, second, and third floors.

The place, in material and in design, looked formidable, safe, and most important to me, quite elegant and clean. The dorms were long with two rows of neatly arranged beds covered by white drapes. However, this ordered situation rapidly deteriorated as people with exhausted bodies and anxious minds rushed in, in a hubbub to secure beds.

At the time of our arrival there was a power outage in the building, so when darkness fell, lanterns and candles were lit to fight off the encamping gloom. Early that night we heard the muffled sound of explosions, and my father assured us that it was the sound of detonated explosives designed and used by the army engineers to breach the river embankment as a necessary flood-control measure to prevent the flooding of the capital. What I did not get at the moment were the consequences of this action. However, being fatigued and sleepy, my eyelids started to flutter. The glow of the lanterns and candles seemed to fade away, and soon I fell into a sound sleep, leaving behind all the uproar and havoc of the world.

In the morning my brother woke me up. Through the nearby window the daylight looked atypical and depressively opaque; the usual opalescence of spring mornings was missing. "Come and have a look," my brother said in an agitated voice. He held my hand and led me upstairs to the uppermost floor. Drowsy, and with faltering steps, I came upon the scene of a scrambled crowd by the tall windows; the ones at the rear stood on tiptoes and craned their necks to look at something that apparently sent them all into tremor. My brother pushed and jostled against the others to finally afford me a footing at one of the windowpanes. I put my hands on the windowsill and eyed the view that faced me. I gasped first, and then I fell into a voiceless stupor. It was an incredible scene, something I'd had no acquaintance with before.

The sky was overcast, but it was not the normal cloudiness that I knew. An amorphous, shadowy mist hung low in the air with a dismal greyness. There was something incomprehensible and bizarre before my eyes! To my great amazement the land had completely disappeared and was replaced by a limitless, turbid, and restlessly writhing waterscape! There was nothing familiar left in sight but murky brown waters choked by all sorts of floating things that had detached from their source and were drifting along. Here and there I could still see the swaying tip of a tree, a reminiscence of the lost world of yesterday, struggling above the brown muddy heaving water. The odd view and the associated chaos carried me to the pinnacle of bewilderment and shock. I involuntarily pressed the hand of my brother.

"Where is our village?" I mumbled in a fear-stricken, hardly audible voice. In response, my brother pointed in a certain direction. As my eyes followed his extended hand, I saw but a watery realm and a dim horizon. There was no trace of the village! The scene was eerie and frightfully alien. I realised that merely overnight, a happening had wiped out all the elements of my familiar world! It was a total and drastic change that I found myself unable to cope with. There was a crawling ague in my body and a twitching in my face, but surprisingly no tears came out of my eyes. I pressed my body against my brother, as if in an effort to regain the departed familiarity and security.

My brother intimately responded by wrapping his arm around my shoulders. "It is all right. It will be all right," he said as we turned our eyes away from the calamitous scene and left the crowd to descend the flight of stairs.

By early afternoon of that day word came, for reasons I cannot remember, to evacuate the building. Soon afterwards, rescue rowboats, accompanied by one or two large motorboats, came to transfer people to another place. Military personnel stood on the stairs that led to the ground floor, which became part of the water world. It was another surprising view when I watched the boats entering from the disjointed windows and doors of the flooded floor. The atmosphere was impregnated with a repellent cadaverous smell, undoubtedly emanating from the heavy floodwater that was littered with all the waste of the ravaged world.

My father helped us board one of the boats. However, because of the prevailing confusion and disorder, we embarked separately, my mother and me in one boat and my brother and sister in another. My father, on the other hand, remained in the building, with other military men, to organise the evacuation of the remaining civilians. The boat, the one I found myself in, oscillated, and I had a difficult time of balancing myself as I struggled to find a space and sit properly. Finally, with the assistance of others, I managed to crouch down and firmly grip the edge of the swaying boat. Neither I nor any other person on board had a life jacket.

The boat finally pulled away from the building. But the situation was far from safe as the boat was filled beyond its capacity. The weighed-down vessel floated with delicate equilibrium, and from my position I realised, with panic, that the murky waters might swamp the boat at any moment. What made matters worse was that some of the people, particularly the elderly, who had found themselves in a boat for the first time in their lives were nervous and disturbingly agitated. Some even attempted to change position in undisciplined, sudden movements, which obliged the corporal, who stood at the bow and was in charge of the boat, to repeatedly shout warnings. Amid this anxiety and apprehension, I heard a collective exclamation of surprise. When I followed the excited eyes, I saw, not very far from our boat, a dog and a cat peacefully sitting on a small drifting bale. The common danger had pacified the two foes. It was a unique sight, but I thought all the happenings that occurred during this wrathful event of nature had their share of dizzying uniqueness. In this unusual state of puzzlement, alert, and fear, my appalled eyes, which wandered erratically from one direction to another, fortuitously came across the other boat, which followed diagonal to us, and there I recognised, to my consternation, Abboud sitting among its occupants! The sight gave me a start, and I felt a new pang of fear and an inward shudder as my worries soared within me. During the few moments during which I gapingly gazed upon the figure, my mind fearfully wondered how on earth he had settled among other people! That looked to be a completely unnatural occurrence! There were abnormalities at every turn, and the world, wreaked in a dizzying havoc, bred aberrant happenings and showered unrelenting calamities! This almost pushed me to weep. But suddenly my shock from seeing Abboud was diverted by another sudden event. I heard a chilling spooky warning bawl from the corporal simultaneous with the sudden movement of a woman who changed her position to cram herself next to me. Instantly, the boat almost capsized. I saw the sky running fast over my head, and eventually I tumbled, face up, into the frothing waters. Seized by a dread of drowning and fear of suffocation, I instinctively struggled to grasp something for dear life and to keep my head up in the air, but I only grasped and flapped about in the water. I inhaled water and found myself drowning when I felt two strong arms encircling my waist and lifting me above the water. With most of my body up in the air, I gasped for air and coughed while many arms extended from the rocking boat to receive me from the rescuer. With a cringing body that dripped water from head to toe, and with a shivering little frame that resembled a tiny bough on a windy day, I crouched, giddy, shocked, and traumatised. Suddenly I started to sob spasmodically, then I burst into a fit of irrepressible weeping. It was then, while being preyed upon by my physical frailty, psychological shock, and emotional disturbance, and with half-awake senses, that I saw, through the veil of tears and drops of water, my saviour: it was Abboud! It was him and no one else!

During that brief moment of identification, I unexpectedly found myself in a state of emotional passivity. I was merely looking at him without a trace of judgement or reaction; it was a rare moment of pure impassiveness as though there equivalent doses of irreconcilable feelings were mixing and merging. I saw his head above the gunnel of the swaying boat. Water trickled profusely down his face, and his blinking eyes watched me closely. I had not seen him before so near, in such close proximity, and what a colossal difference that made, for there came an unwavering, surprising, and quite confusing recognition: his eyes were sparkling with tenderness, goodness, and clemency.

Postflood

As displaced people, we spent the following two months in a tent camp in the al-Washash district on the western side of the Tigris River. During that time I had no idea what was going on in the flooded area and particularly our village, but sometime in July or August, and while the relocated people were suffering from the scorching, unbearable heat and the occasional strong dust storms that often dislodged the pegs of tents and caused lots of trouble for the families, we were advised to get ready to return to our village. So, in the midmorning of one bright day we travelled in a packed bus, and in one hour's time or so we arrived at our destination.

When I set my eyes on the place, I found myself incapable of recognising things, the village having been totally demolished with buildings replaced by shapeless mounds of clay with wooden logs jutting up here and there. Dense shrubs and bushes erupted from the ground in riot to mask, with uncommon greenery, the formless subdued undulations that marked the collapsed dwellings. After some time and effort, I became able to orient myself thanks to the few stationary landmarks that had survived the disaster, strictly the line of date palms and the big eucalyptus tree.

From the first day of their return, the flood-stricken people started to remove the detritus and subsequently commenced, with bare hands, to rebuild their homes—an activity that transformed the location into a huge, unprecedented workshop. Houses gradually emerged. At first there were sporadic abodes with wide interspersed spaces, then slowly but progressively the vacant land strips shrank and houses coalesced. The village finally acquired an almost identical appearance to that of the preflood time except for the new fresh aspect. The last touch to the reconstruction process was the rebuilding of the village school, a task that had been achieved by the collective work of the people. The completion of this last work almost perfected my psychological harmony with the postflood world, and I felt that life in the resurrected milieu had regained its normal beats.

One day I stood at the doorway of the house, which still lacked a door and windows. The air was utterly dull and oppressively hot. Being subjected to blazing sunlight, the land had a glare that made the eyes ache. I raised my hand to shade my eyes from the harsh glow as I looked at the monotonously flat terrain. On the western horizon there was a mercurial heat haze, a gleaming mirage that danced above the dark line of shrubs that littered the extended plain. As I turned my eyes eastward, I caught sight of the lofty eucalyptus tree. For more than a week, I'd had an importunate yet latent urge to be near the gigantic tree. Yet I did not go there, because I was totally occupied with my family in the painstaking task of rebuilding our home. However, during all that time, my subconscious was working clandestinely. It wove a conscious dolorous association between the tree and an unsettling issue of conscience as I had a grinding feeling of guilt mixed with shame related to my behaviour towards Abboud that kept panging and goading me. And because of this lurking moral process, there developed a change inside me, a metamorphosis in my heart and mind that bore the signs of early adolescence. Now, as I stood free from the physical labour with slurry, my feelings of being a doer of iniquity became more pronounced and crystalline with an urging and gnawing call to make it up to Abboud and to fix things with him.

The sun was at its zenith, and I stood at the doorstep, gazing towards the giant tree. From a distance it appeared as if nothing had touched its pride. Then, suddenly, I felt an irresistible and importunate urge to climb it. I moved my feet, and within few minutes I found myself at the foot of the enormous trunk. Contrary to my first impression, and on closer inspection, I recognised that the tree did bear certain marks of suffering and showed wounds caused by the devastating flood. The bark had been largely removed from the lower part of the trunk, and the lowest branches and twigs had broken off and been carried away. Buoyed up by the nibbling moral impulse to see the lenient, introverted man who saved my life, and more importantly by the impulse to redress my past misconduct and to right a wrong, I set my hands and feet on the sturdy torso and eagerly started my ascent. But immediately I found scaling the trunk was more arduous than I had ever experienced before. And no wonder, as the acquired smoothness of the tree body rendered it slippery and I had to rely on the few rough locations of severed branches and subtle cracks as leverage points for my hands and feet. I used my maximum might, stamina, and climbing dexterity as my sweating hands had a weak grip while my bare feet unsteadily and erratically shifted position in search of a secure foothold to avoid a slip. I inched my way upward and made a piecemeal ascent up this formidable grand mast of nature, while my emotional objective fuelled me with sufficient sedulity to meet the physical challenge. Fatigued and sweating, I finally set my hands and feet on the large curved branch. For a few moments, I sat there motionlessly to gather my breath and to quieten the thumping beats in my chest. In tune with the somnolent dull atmosphere, the tree stood inanimate, not manifesting the feeblest pulse. No twig shook and no leaf stirred. There was lethargic dormancy and inertness galore. The dominant silence was only broken by the occasional scratchy sound of cicadas prowling among the thorny shrubs or by the sudden flutter of sparrow wings. As I looked around, I found the surrounding world less picturesque than before. It was insipid, tame scenery where many elements were missing, or rather had disappeared. The flood had wiped out many features, among them the irrigation canal, the oleander bushes, the willow trees, and the cavalry stables. The spectacular trapezoid earth hill had been transformed into a large formless mound of clay surrounded by dense grassy vegetation.

On the rough hanging seat of nature, I sat with elbows resting on my raised knees. I propped my head up with my hands and looked, with anticipation, at the dusty road that was now bounded by chaotic, matted scrubs and thorny bushes. "He will show up at any moment," I mumbled to myself as I believed Abboud's daily one-way journey was one of the constants of nature! Time passed, and I waited and watched, yet the route remained empty. With intense appeal I strained my eyes, but there was no sign of him as far as my sight could see.

Then, after one hour or so of fruitless waiting, I finally gave up and climbed down with a heavy heart. The next day I climbed again and waited for a longer time, but I reaped the same disappointment. And with that questions started to whirl in my mind: *Where is he? Why hasn't he shown up?* On the following days I tenaciously continued climbing the enormous tree. I watched and wove hope, but nothing happened; there was no trace of him. So, after those days of unfruitful waiting, I bitterly realised that the opportunity to make amends to Abboud for my misconduct seemed to be vitiated and lost.

Up till that time, my mind intuitively took permanence for granted; I thought irrevocability was an inherent feature of life. I took it as axiomatic that elements of the world, people and things alike, had continuity and persistence. But now I perceived the fact that there was no everlastingness, that things were bound to undergo irreversible change, and this recognition brought me a vague sadness. My heartache and compunction grew steadily as I obscurely came to realise that Abboud and his routine might have become a relic, a memory from a past that could be neither resurrected nor enlivened again—a realisation that tossed me into a slowly growing melancholy. I became gradually morose and sombre with quietness and silence progressively depicting my everyday behaviour, which flagrantly contrasted with my normal obstreperous, rowdy ways and my hyperactivity. This change in personality and behaviour, though slow and incremental, did not escape the notice of my family. It became a subject for humour, which brought me soreness and embarrassment, but surprisingly no anger.

I remember particularly well my last climbing of the eucalyptus tree, which had more emotional context than any incentive of real hope. I sat on the tree branch with my knees up. I crossed my legs at the ankles and folded my hands loosely around the raised knees while my upper body imperceptibly swayed back and forth. As I looked at the faraway eastern horizon, where the celestial ceiling leant on the earth, I fancied seeing the visage of Abboud occupying the whole view, framed by the uttermost limits of earth and sky; it was the kind face that I closely looked at the last and only time. Yes, in that still space of high noon, the outlines of his countenance came distinct, clear, and lively. I saw his soaked, dripping hair where the falling drops coalesced into minute rills that ran down his solemn face. There was also the reassuring smile and the twinkling eyes that shone with goodness. But the image did not stay long, just a few moments. Soon it became blurry and melted away in the pool of my silent tears.

Two Worlds[1]

It was a rainy evening. The city[2] lights rendered the wet ground shimmering with iridescent shades. Nearly midway down Boulevard Anspach, a brasserie occupied the corner made with a side street. The place was a rectangular hall. One side was a half glass wall that overlooked a narrow street. The other long side was a wood-covered wall that lent a rural feeling. But in dissonance with this rustic design, two oversized copies of Magritte paintings occupied the middle of the space. It was warm and quiet inside, and the trapped air rippled with a soft piano melody, "O sole mio". There were very few customers: two men at the bar, and a couple occupying a table beside the solid wall. Across, on the other side, a wheatish-skinned man sat at a small table, sipping from a cup of coffee while watching the erratic path of raindrops on the large glass pane, which also revealed the fuzzy figures of the few hurried passers-by. The entrance door briefly opened, and with that the sound of rain impinging on the corrugated plastic awning penetrated the brasserie

---

[1] Written as a birthday gift for Heide Mittermayer.
[2] Brussels.

147

room. The new customer helped herself off with her overcoat, hung it on the hanger, and sat down. The man with the dark complexion turned his head and looked at the newcomer, who had just taken a nearby seat. Her sheath dress exposed a curvy figure, and her long ginger hair crowned her milky white face. But it was her eyes that were of particular gravity to him: they were deep, deep blue. "Heavens! I have never seen eyes with such shade of blue! The lure of spellbinding seas!" He sighed.

The woman was attentive to the piercing gaze of her neighbour and cast upon him a coquettish look while entertaining a pleasurable thought: *This is a man full of prurient desires.* She crossed her legs and beckoned to the waiter. The watching man flipped through the pages of a book he had on the table and took out a neatly folded paper. Then he took a ballpoint pen from his inner jacket pocket. *No dissimulation of exquisite sentiment.* He excused himself as he persistently meditated upon the singularity of those two patches of blue that caused a lofty joy to well up from his soul. The waiter neared the woman and winked; she uttered a few words, and he left. She glanced back at the solemn neighbour. *Is he going to approach me?* she wishfully thought.

At that moment, another melody was playing, "Les feuilles mortes", and outside the rain relentlessly poured with an occasional celestial roar. The agile waiter came back with a glass of white wine and set it down on the coaster. The woman nudged him with her elbow and smiled. The man, who was occasionally moving his pen on the blank paper, watched this brief scene with a tight-lipped expression. The waiter went back to the bar and whispered something to a portly person sitting there, who immediately turned around, revealing a red, sagging face. He briefly explored the woman with his eyes and quaffed from his glass the remaining liquor. He walked with short strides across the space separating them to stand next to her and look down with promiscuous eyes. Still holding the glass of wine in her hand, she glanced at him from head to toe and smiled. Without further ado, he pulled up a chair and sat. The couple talked in a low voice for a while, and finally the woman jiggled and poked the man's flabby belly with her forefinger. The bulky man stood up, walked back towards the bar, paid the grinning waiter, and returned to where the woman was standing akimbo. He hooked his arm in hers, and they left. Discomfited, the solo man dropped his pen on the table. He rubbed his shiny raven hair and looked through the glass pane to the blurry world outside, lost in thought. A bolt of lightning flashed, followed by far-off muffled thunder. The waiter came whistling to clear the table where the woman had been sitting. The man turned his head and looked with brooding eyes. The waiter exchanged glances with him and nodded at the empty place. "What fun!" he said with a sly smile.

"Nonsense! No real fun in life, but disillusionment!" the starry-eyed man said in a sombre tone. Then he shifted his eyes to stare back down at the paper laying on the table. He held it for a moment then crumpled it in his right hand.

Printed in the United States
By Bookmasters